WATERY GRAVE

SEAL Brotherhood: Legacy Series
Book 1

SHARON HAMILTON

SHARON HAMILTON'S BOOK LIST

SEAL BROTHERHOOD BOOKS

SEAL BROTHERHOOD SERIES
Accidental SEAL Book 1
Fallen SEAL Legacy Book 2
SEAL Under Covers Book 3
SEAL The Deal Book 4
Cruisin' For A SEAL Book 5
SEAL My Destiny Book 6
SEAL of My Heart Book 7
Fredo's Dream Book 8
SEAL My Love Book 9
SEAL Encounter Prequel to Book 1
SEAL Endeavor Prequel to Book 2
Ultimate SEAL Collection Vol. 1 Books 1-4 /2 Prequels
Ultimate SEAL Collection Vol. 2 Books 5-7

SEAL BROTHERHOOD LEGACY SERIES
Watery Grave Book 1

BAD BOYS OF SEAL TEAM 3 SERIES
SEAL's Promise Book 1
SEAL My Home Book 2
SEAL's Code Book 3
Big Bad Boys Bundle Books 1-3

BAND OF BACHELORS SERIES
Lucas Book 1
Alex Book 2
Jake Book 3

Jake 2 Book 4
Big Band of Bachelors Bundle

BONE FROG BROTHERHOOD SERIES
New Year's SEAL Dream Book 1
SEALed At The Altar Book 2
SEALed Forever Book 3
SEAL's Rescue Book 4
SEALed Protection Book 5

SUNSET SEALS SERIES
SEALed at Sunset
Second Chance SEAL
Treasure Island SEAL
Escape to Sunset
The House at Sunset Beach

SILVER SEALS SERIES
SEAL Love's Legacy

SLEEPER SEALS SERIES
Bachelor SEAL

BONE FROG BACHELOR SERIES
Bone Frog Bachelor
Unleashed

STAND ALONE BOOKS & SERIES
SEAL's Goal: The Beautiful Game
Nashville SEAL: Jameson
True Blue SEALS Zak
Paradise: In Search of Love
Love Me Tender, Love You Hard

All of Sharon's books are available on Audible,
narrated by the talented J.D. Hart.

ABOUT THE BOOK

Christy and Kyle Lansdowne receive a long-lost piece of luggage returned from a cruise vacation from Hell several years prior. Inside, lies the remains of SEAL Team 3 friend and former gym owner, Joseph "Gunny" Hoskins. Their mission was to release his ashes upon the deep blue sea, but their cruise was interrupted by a terrorist takeover of the ship, thwarted by the SEALs on board.

But when the ocean returns him to San Diego in Christy's cosmetic bag, a new adventure is hatched to give Gunny eternal rest.

Kyle, Christy and their three children embark on another memorial cruise mission, along with several other SEAL families. In paying tribute to the life of a fellow brother-in-arms, they usher in the dawn of a bright new future for them all. As the past is finally buried amid the dangers of the present, the ocean's giant wheel—the Circle of Life—lives on.

In honoring the irreverent life of one, the bond and commitment of the brothers who remain is strengthened to do battle.

SEAL Brotherhood: Legacy Series is about the original couples in Sharon's popular SEAL Brotherhood Series. It furthers the stories of these couples ten years later, after marriages, children and separations. These are stand alone books, but readers who are unfamiliar with the series would enjoy reading the background stories first.

AUTHOR'S NOTE

I always dedicate my SEAL Brotherhood books to the brave men and women who defend our shores and keep us safe. Without their sacrifice, and that of their families—because a warrior's fight always includes his or her family—I wouldn't have the freedom and opportunity to make a living writing these stories. They sometimes pay the ultimate price so we can debate, argue, go have coffee with friends, raise our children and see them have children of their own.

One of my favorite tributes to warriors resides on many memorials, including one I saw honoring the fallen of WWII on an island in the Pacific:

> "When you go home
> Tell them of us, and say
> For your tomorrow,
> We gave our today."

These are my stories created out of my own imagination. Anything that is inaccurately portrayed is either my mistake, or done intentionally to disguise something I might have overheard over a beer or in the corner of one of the hangouts along the Coronado Strand.

I support two main charities. Navy SEAL/UDT Museum operates in Ft. Pierce, Florida. Please learn about this wonderful museum, all run by active and former SEALs and their friends and families, and who rely on public support, not that of the U.S. Government. www.navysealmuseum.org

IF YOU GOT ANY CLOSER, YOU WOULD HAVE TO ENLIST

I also support Wounded Warriors, who tirelessly bring together the warrior as well as the family members who are just learning to deal with their soldier's condition and have nowhere to turn. It is a long path to becoming well, but I've seen first-hand what this organization does for its warriors and the families who love them. Please give what your heart tells you is right. If you cannot give, volunteer at one of the many service centers all over the United States. Get involved. Do something meaningful for someone who gave so much of themselves, to families who have paid the price for your freedom. You'll find a family there unlike any other on the planet. www.woundedwarriorproject.org

CHAPTER 1

I T WAS A beautiful Spring day in Coronado when Davey Jones barfed up one of his special ones. Kyle had just put the two boys in a corner for their second time out of the day when the doorbell rang. Luke, the youngest of their three, had managed to develop quite an uppercut. He'd split and fattened his older brother's upper lip, which protruded forward like a bad Botox treatment.

Brandon was deadly with the cusswords he'd learned before Kyle and Christy became aware of it and started paying attention to their home language, and he demonstrated his skills for everyone in the house. But Luke was the silent type and nearly fearless—a biproduct of being the youngest. Unlike his older siblings, his first word was "mine."

Kyle was secretly proud of both of them but had to hide it in front of Christy and the boys. Maggie as well, whom he considered his incredible, fearless warrior princess. Luckily, Christy was at work, driving around a newbie SEAL and his girlfriend, checking out houses they wouldn't be able to afford unless someone came from big bucks, which happened never.

When Kyle opened the front door, a cloud of moisture from his lawn sprinklers gently bathed his face. He came face-to-face with a twenty-something goth kid with a wooden ear plug the size of a quarter, wearing eye makeup and clutching a faded tote bag with flower and heart stickers all over it.

California has really gone to the dogs.

He almost slammed the door in the kid's face but saddled his patience and eked out a smile.

"Is there a Christy Lansdowne who lives here?" he asked.

"That would be my wife," Kyle said, his eyes squinting, ready to clock the kid on his doorstep.

"I'm from Crown and Star Cruise Lines, and we're returning her lost luggage."

Kyle hesitated before he took hold of the hot pink handle. Now he recognized Christy's cosmetic bag, the one they'd taken with them on the cruise some ten years ago when they'd thwarted a terrorist attack aboard ship. Another bag had been returned almost a year ago now. But this one was special. It contained the ashes of one Joseph Hoskins, better known to Team 3 as "Gunny"—their former Marine brother-in-arms and owner of Gunny's Gym, where they worked out. Their mission had been to return Gunny to the sea.

When the bags were lost, the Team figured the terrorists took care of that detail for them. They'd held their service anyhow, without the spreading of the ashes, which had been lost in the mayhem that ensued.

The case was still heavy. Kyle rattled it a bit to see if it was still filled with water. He just heard dry contents jostling around.

"We make sure they don't leak when we bring them back. It's been sitting at our warehouse in Florida for at least a year, so I'd tell your missus not to use any of the makeup."

The kid must not have known about the contents.

"There's a dead man inside," Kyle said, his voice an ominous, raspy whisper, imitating a pirate.

The messenger jumped back about three inches. "Geez. I didn't know that. I didn't *need* to know that."

With his hands shaking, he produced a wilted consent form and a ballpoint pen, asking for a signature and indicating where. Kyle ripped it out of his hands, set down the case unceremoniously, and scribbled a signature no one would be able to read, shoving it back into the kid's chest.

"You have yourself a good day, son." He winked and then slammed the door.

The boys had heard too much of the conversation,

especially the part about the dead guy inside, and came running over. Surrounding Kyle, they jumped up and down and peppered him with questions. Maggie tried to grab the case.

Kyle ran through the living room, the case high above his head, with his three children jumping up to try to grab it from his fingers. He was laughing so hard he nearly lost his focus when Maggie almost snatched it.

"Wait a minute, guys!" he yelled, setting the case down on the kitchen countertop. He knew Christy would be horrified to see it there, but he had no choice. Finally, to keep the kids from leaping over the top of the counter, he had to raise his voice another few decibels.

"Cut it out. Stop! This is enough!"

They knew he was at the end of his rope.

"I'm going to open it, slowly. But I'm not sure it's healthy for you to be close, so back off! And I mean it, dammit!"

Behind him, he heard Christy's voice. "So why is that thing even in my kitchen, Kyle?"

He whirled around to find the disapproving face of his beloved, her face wrinkled in a scowl. Her right shoulder dipped slightly lower than the left, pulled down by the weight of a computer strap and case hanging below.

It was one of those cat-and-canary moments. He'd been caught, almost anticipated he'd been caught.

"This just arrived!" He pointed to the dirty case fouling her kitchen.

"I should hope so. I mean, wouldn't want that hanging around all day. Whatever possessed you to tell the kids you were going to open it? Here?"

He really didn't have an answer for that one. Ask him anything about freefalling from thirteen thousand feet or firepower from different caliber ammo, and he'd have answers at the ready. But this, well, he'd never trained for this.

"So you'd prefer I take this to the backyard?" He reached for the bag, but Christy slapped his hand away.

"I'd prefer that you blew it up."

"Cool!" Brandon said quickly and then realized his mistake. One glare from Christy, and the boys were exceedingly quiet. But Maggie took on the challenge.

"Can I light it up?" she asked, a devilish grin crossing her face.

Kyle shook his head. What had he taught his little brood?

"Nope. We're going to take a look at this in private and you kids aren't going to be anywhere near it." She dropped her computer bag, grabbed a tea towel, used it to pick up the handle, and, holding it out away from her body like a poop-soaked dirty diaper, headed for the back door. Before she stepped over the threshold, she abruptly turned, all three children piling up on one another as they stopped. "*No one* comes outside. And *everyone* washes their hands and face."

No one moved. Even Kyle wasn't sure what to do.

"I said *now*, troops! You march yourselves into the bathroom and wash those hands and faces before I stick you all in the tub together!"

This, of course, was always threatened, especially the part about the boys having to stand or sit naked in the tub or shower with their sister, but never really happened. Yet it worked every time. The boys were going through a "girls have cooties" phase that Kyle knew would last a few years before morphing into something more dangerous.

The three of them disappeared down the hallway. Kyle heard water splashing and the beginnings of an argument while he followed Christy outside.

"Honestly, Kyle. I thought you had better sense about hazmat things," Christy was barking as he followed her. "You have no idea if this could be dangerous."

"Honey, they wouldn't deliver it if it was. I'm thinking—"

"No, Kyle, you weren't thinking, because if you were, you'd have stayed outside with this little IED and not brought it into **our** house and expose the kids. If it was a package in a plain brown paper wrapping, you wouldn't touch it, right?"

She did have a point there.

"But—"

"I know, I know. It has flowers and heart stickers all over it, and you recognized it as being mine. But would you take a look at this piece of shit?" She held the case up until satisfied Kyle understood the full import of her wrath.

"You're right, Christy. Of course, you're right. I wasn't thinking."

Satisfied, she set the bag on the glass-top table on their patio under the opened red umbrella. Stepping back one pace, she examined it.

"I already shook it," Kyle added, trying to be helpful.

"Of course you did. And you're still here. So I'm guessing it's just what we thought, but I still don't know what to do about opening it."

"Let me call Fredo. He'll know about explosives and—"

"And I want another opinion too."

"Well, I think Coop should be available. We could use a medic. Maybe Lucas or Jake. Tucker might know a thing or two about it. T.J.?"

"Sure. You call some boys over here. I'm going to call the funeral parlor where he was fried."

Kyle winced at Christy's words. It was hardly fitting for the honor and respect he held for the man who, if their hunch was correct, might still be residing inside this pink case. Christy was serious, dropping the tea towel on the table and slapping her hands together as if getting rid of Gunny's dust and ashes. It was slightly irreverent, Kyle thought.

"How was *your* day, sweetie?" he asked.

"Don't ask. A disaster. I'm referring them out. Next time, I'm not taking any more of you guys until you are good and married. I think he just wanted to impress her about living here in sunny San Diego so he could get a good lay tonight. Honestly, these newbies are not like the original."

She frowned, shaking her pretty blonde hair from side to side. Her slim body poured into the white linen suit, the skirt just a little tight over her beautiful, perfect ass. In high heels and bone-colored stockings, she always took his breath away, especially when she was irritated. He loved the flushed, warm feeling she exhibited when he smiled at her and, without words, told her he was damned happy she was his wife of eleven years.

She approached, eyes downcast, allowing his attraction to grow. She stopped as her thighs scraped against his, her arms up over his shoulders, leaning forward until her tits pressed against his chest. "I can't leave you alone for one afternoon without some big adventure befalling us?"

"But you left me alone with three hellions, Christy. And we didn't do the deed this morning before you left. That's always a bad sign. Next time, let me take you in the shower like I started to before you realized you were running late." He kissed her softly then went back for a deep one, feeling her melt into him.

"But I was running late," she sighed, kissing him back.

"I love it when we have to be quick. I like it urgent and bare."

"Oh, you do, do you? So is that why you turned off my phone?"

"I did. I had plans. And you were stronger than I was."

"I'm never stronger than you are, Kyle." She brushed her fingers over his lips. He palmed her left buttock and pressed her against his package.

"So I could take you right here and you couldn't resist me?" he whispered in her ear, chewing on her earlobe.

"Not with that thing staring at us!" she barked and pointed to the case.

Kyle dropped his arms and sighed. "Now we're back to that, and I was just getting the biggest hard-on of my week."

She winked at him and then was all business. "Go make your calls, lover boy. I'll make sure the kids turn in early tonight, and you can have your way with me in the hot tub. How's that?"

"Works for me!"

CHAPTER 2

A TEAM OF eight men stood with Kyle around the patio table, gazing down at the pink case that had mysteriously shown up to Kyle and Christy's house. No one touched it, instead treating it like an object or projectile from Outer Space.

"I'm going to be totally honest with you, Kyle," Fredo said, rubbing his chin. "You need to blow this thing up. I don't know if it's safe or lethal." The height-challenged SEAL didn't resemble his giant brothers on the team, but his heart was fierce. And, because he was an explosives expert, it was his answer to everything.

"Seriously, Kyle. I don't think Gunny would mind," added Trace. "If he's looking down on us right now, he's laughing his ass off."

There was some agreement within the group, quietly expressed.

Calvin Cooper, Fredo's best friend, made another suggestion. "Can we borrow one of SDPD's X-ray units? Maybe get a peek inside? They have one they use for bomb threats. We could—"

He was interrupted by T.J. Talbot. "No way they'd let you X-ray that thing. Maybe soak it down with water? Dunk it in an abandoned pool or something to make sure it isn't flammable?"

"And then contaminate the pool and kill any kid or animal who came near it? How would we go about draining the water, and where would we put it? Just creates a bigger problem," answered Kyle.

Tucker had a suggestion. "Call the funeral home. Ask them what happens to ashes that are that old, if there's any pressure buildup in the urn. I kinda doubt it, though."

"Christy's on the phone with them now. From the sounds of it, no one wants to stick their neck out to tell her anything. Health and Safety issues, it appears."

Fredo and Tucker both had a chuckle over that one.

"Oh sure, they do the toasty thing and get them up to—what?—two thousand degrees?" Fredo barked. "Ten years later, they better hope nothing survived and became lethal. But just to be sure, they don't want to say. It's in an urn, for Chrissakes!"

"But they have a plug at the bottom that screws open," added Jason Kealoha. "When I took Thomas to the Gulf, it was pretty airtight but no pressure. I unscrewed it, and the wind took it all away. I think you're safe. More than likely, it's muddy sludge, even after all these years."

"You would think they would have opened the case and looked inside. I would have," said Danny Begay. He shuddered. "I don't want to touch that thing. The Dine don't like ashes or dead bodies. I'm going with my ancestors on this one, Kyle."

Kyle shrugged. Each man had his private and public thoughts. They all took turns commenting on what should be done as Christy appeared at the back screen door and opened it. Kyle's three kids stood behind, faces plastered into the grid, watching their mom.

Her long, shapely legs were now fitted into a comfortable, stretchy pair of leggings. A sloppy top nearly hung down to her knees. With her blonde hair scrunched up in a clip, she headed directly for the bag in her bare feet, filled with attitude and purpose, almost appearing angry. Her red nail polish sparkled in the late afternoon sun.

The crowd of muscled warriors in front of her separated without a word, like drops of oil in a glass of water.

She leaned over the table and grabbed the bag. Before Kyle could yank it away from her, she unclasped the lock using her combination code and opened the lid like slicing the top of a man's skull and peeling it back. Her red nails dug inside, and out she pulled the much-tarnished steel tube engraved with a Trident on the front. It was about the size of a small milkshake at the Scupper. She held it over her head and shook it like she was mixing a martini.

The men looked on in shocked horror.

Nobody came for her, so she eyed them all and shook the contents again, which rattled as if it was filled with pieces of small rocks and topsoil. With a devilish grin, she began to twist open the container, and immediately, Kyle and T.J. were all over her. T.J. yanked the container away as Kyle held her back several feet, but she tried to resist, without luck.

Several of the men guffawed. "Remind me where you got your courage, Christy?" T.J. mumbled.

"She's been holding out on us," added Cooper.

"Holy smoke!" swore Fredo.

"And that's exactly what we got here. These are genuine Joseph Hoskins ashes all right," T.J. said as he poured part of the chunky grey mixture on the table. Little clusters had formed in the ash, several looking like tiny rosebuds. T.J. wrinkled his nose, prepared to smell something he'd live to regret. He re-secured the bottom plug. A tiny gust of wind picked up the remains in a whirlwind and drove some light grey ash toward Heaven, as if it had been divinely ordained.

Three of the members crossed themselves. Someone swore, and Tucker, who had been in the path of the cloud as it was moving, brushed his shirt off and rubbed his hair free of anything lingering.

"Goddammit," he mumbled, displeased. "I'm gonna need a fuckin' shower before I can walk through my own front door."

Fredo examined the contents on the table. "That's kinda chunky, don't you think? Are those pieces of his pacemaker or something?"

"They take those out. Nuclear waste," barked T.J. But he too was examining the grey clumps.

"Maybe teeth?" asked Fredo.

Christy wiggled free from Kyle's grip and addressed the team, her hands on her hips. "And you guys are in charge of keeping this country safe. Look at all of you, afraid of a little bit of ash, the remains from a friend."

"Well, that's the point, Christy," said Coop. "We wanted to make sure it was safe. We weren't afraid. And it was out of respect for Gunny. Even though Fredo here wanted to blow him up."

"Again," said several others in unison.

"What's this clumpy stuff?" Danny repeated the earlier question, his face reflecting disgust.

"How did you get the balls to do that?" Fredo asked.

Christy smiled, relishing the moment she knew was going to quickly pass. "When no one at the funeral home had an answer, I figured it was no biggie. And I remember studying about an ancient dig in Egypt, where remains were found in clay pots and stored for thousands of years. You actually thought his ashes would explode?"

"Kinda makes me glad we didn't go asking for the X-ray machine," whispered Coop.

"No kidding," answered Kyle.

"But I still want to know how come it looks like that. Is that from the sea water getting into it?" persisted Danny.

Christy grinned. "I added potpourri so it would go through customs, just in case they tried to open it."

There was a collective "ah" as the mystery of the grey, chunky matter was solved.

"So now what?" asked Trace. "We bury him all over again?"

T.J. re-poured the remaining ash back into the cylinder and screwed it shut again. He set it down next to the ridiculous-looking pink camo cosmetic case with the stickers all over it, including some smiley faces and many smiley hearts. Wiping his hands on his jeans, he continued, "I say we're in for a do-over. We pick a date before our next workup and see if we can get one of those cheap five-day cruises from San Diego to somewhere along Baja—maybe Cabo? We release old Gunny to the whale migration lanes along the Pacific."

"I'm for that. Something cheap and simple. We could take the wives, the kids, make it a Team vacation. Some of us didn't get to do it the first time around," said Trace.

"No, we're not going to do it that way again!" Coop argued, referring to how the first attempt went south. He had his arms folded across his chest. "But I think Libby would love a cruise, and the kids would too. They're old enough to enjoy a boat trip."

"Then it's settled. I'll get word out so we know how many we are, and I'll get with the agent who booked us before, if she's still around," said Kyle. He walked over to Christy, grabbing her around the waist and planting a big kiss on her cheek. He nuzzled her ear and whispered just loud enough for the team to hear, "And God knows we could use a small cabin space while the kids are preoccupied."

Jake, who was paying alimony and child support to two former wives plus supporting four kids that he knew of, spoke his peace. "Make sure it's cheap, okay? If I'm bringing Ginger and the two girls, I can't afford two rooms. We'll all be packed in there like sardines. Either that, or I can't go."

"You bringing Karlene or Monica too?" asked Fredo.

"Oh, like that would go over really well with Ginger, you dumb fuck," Jake dished back.

"Fredo!" shouted Christy. "You're a married man!"

But the comment hung in the air, unanswered. Jake's ex, Karlene, was still unmarried and had been a serial dater of many of the single SEALs on Team 3. There had been a healthy rivalry developing amongst the men over who would finally win her over. Monica, whom Jake never married but had a daughter with, was considered too hot to handle, and the single guys stayed away.

Kyle growled. "Jake doesn't need any more problems, Fredo. If he brings Ginger and the girls, just remember we're going to *Mexico*. There's a certain General Cortez looking for him, so I doubt Jake will be doing much sightseeing."

"Kyle," T.J. started, "I think we *all* could use a little Team bonding right about now. This is as good an excuse as any, wouldn't you say? And anyhow, wouldn't it be a good idea to put the memory of that last cruise out of everyone's mind and replace it with a nice, relaxing boating excursion along the Mexican Riviera?"

"It could be just the thing we need right now." Kyle was convinced.

"Just the sun, the sea, and our wives. The kids can run like a pack of wolves and get into trouble we don't have to see. I think it would be a blast," T.J. whispered, handing Christy the cannister with a wink. "What could be better?"

CHAPTER 3

THERE WERE FIFTY-THREE of them by the time they added everybody in, and Christy was going nuts, just trying to keep her room assignments straight. They had requested everyone be housed in the same section of the ship, but since some wanted to get bigger state rooms than others, others wanted balconies, and a few wanted interior suites, it was a minefield to figure out. In the end, she did a pretty good job of keeping people happy and paying what they could afford. In a couple of cases, she and Kyle helped along some of the single SEALs who had not built up their savings. Newbie SEALs usually went out and bought brand-new trucks or SUVs, and odds were good they would be repossessed within the first year.

Due to the number of children coming with them, this particular itinerary and ship were made for families. It wasn't a heavy drinking crowd, although most cruise ships turned into that, nonetheless. They had a huge children's section, including a three-story tree house, outdoor water slides, and all sorts of events run by cruise staff members that the couples could take advantage of to find a little bit of personal alone time and to dine at some of the seven world-class restaurants on board. The ship was brand new. Though not one of the largest ships in the fleet, this was one of its very first runs. It would be spending the rest of the year, the winter months, in South America or doing the transatlantic tours.

Kyle and the three little Lansdownes followed behind Christy as she searched the hallway, looking for their room. She had booked a little extra space with a wider balcony, and it included a bunk bed. One of the kids would have to sleep on the couch or with her and Kyle.

Kyle was trying to keep the boys from ganging up on Maggie. Since Brandon was older than she was, he claimed the top bunk. But Luke was vying for a bunk, too, which left Maggie out completely. It was already looking like she'd probably be sleeping with her and Kyle.

"Would you just quit it?" screamed Maggie. Trying another tactic, she complained to her dad. "Brandon is stepping on the back of my heels, Dad. I want you to tell him to stop."

"Brandon, you heard Maggie. What's got into

you?" Kyle barked.

"I didn't do it. *Luke* did."

Luke piped up immediately to defend himself, screaming, "That's not fair. You're lying Brandon. You are a fucking liar!"

That got Christy's attention. She dropped her bags, turned around, and grabbed both Brandon and Luke by their ears, even though Brandon came up to mid chest level on her. But she pulled them aside and spoke to them, her face not more than two inches from the front of theirs.

"I'll not have that language on this vacation, do you hear? If you're gonna talk like that, I'll have your dad fly you two home, and Maggie and I will have a nice vacation."

Both boys squirmed, not liking the pressure she was applying to the upper cartilage of their ears.

"I'm going to say this one more time, boys, and then I'm just going to let your dad do the corporal punishment thing. Now you know what that means, and he doesn't spank lightly like I do. You won't be able to sit down for the entire cruise if you don't stop giving each other trouble. And it's not fair on all the rest of us. Your dad's the leader of this group. We are supposed to act like a model family, the family everyone's supposed to emulate. You got it?"

"Yes, ma'am," the boys said in unison.

"I'm going to reduce your amount of playtime or swim time by single digits starting tonight. Then tomorrow, if your behavior doesn't get any better, I'm going to double that. And if you're not really careful, you're going to be eating hot dogs and potato chips in the room every day and not having any playtime. Now if you think sitting around and watching TV all day sounds like fun, just consider one thing. There are only three channels on the ship, plus the closed-circuit feed and the shopping channel. One of them is an animal documentary series. You can also pick Chinese business TV or BBC news."

She didn't think that either boy knew what that meant, but their little noses were scrunched up anyway. It wasn't their normal fare of cartoons, action films, or music videos. She could see the threat had somewhat of an impact on them.

"But what if Maggie starts it? She sometimes does little things that just push my buttons," said Luke.

Christy could see Kyle cover his mouth in her peripheral vision, secretly wanting to break out in a laugh, because little Luke repeated the words with the same tonality as his father did from time to time. Luke was a carbon copy of his old man.

"You bring it to my attention then. That's what you do," she encouraged him.

"Yes, ma'am," the boys said in unison again.

Christy turned to her daughter. "Maggie? They're going to be looking for all kinds of ways that you're violating the rules, and they're going to try to get even if you try anything. Don't let them. I want you to be a perfect angel. Can you do that?"

She smiled, showing a huge gap between her front upper teeth. Luke had lost his a year ago, and they'd already grown back in, but Maggie's teeth were considerably slower. "Yes, ma'am. I sure can." She looked at her brothers, angling her head and giving them a satisfied grimace.

Christy slid by Kyle, making full body contact with his chest. He tried to grab her but missed. She picked up her bags and mumbled to herself all the way down the hallway, counting rooms on the left until they came to the end of the passageway. A corner door led to a double compartment suite, which wasn't their room, but they had the cabin next door with an equally large balcony. She set the key in the slot, and the door clicked open, the lights inside turning on immediately.

The kids overran both of them, heading for the sliding glass door while Kyle and Christy laid their suitcases on the bed. The kids stood trying to jiggle the handle, until Brandon figured out that he had to remove a pin in order to pull the door back. They hopped out onto the balcony and leaned over the railing. Christy could hear their squeals and conversation, each of them pointing out things along the pier, as well as pointing to people above and below them hanging out over their own balconies.

Christy looked up into the eyes of her handsome husband. "I can't believe I willingly walked into this," she whispered, her voice husky and purposely inviting. She was tired from all the preparations, the anticipation, and the worry she'd forgotten something or someone. It was ever a problem for the wife of a Team Leader, especially one as well respected by his men as Kyle.

"Babe, it had to be. And no one but you could have pulled this whole thing off, right from the moment you grabbed Gunny from the bowels of your bag." Kyle chuckled as he drew her against him. "Look at it this way," he said as he began to kiss her neck, feeling and squeezing her buttocks through her pants. "You might get breakfast in bed several times, and you never get that at home. The kids will be occupied a whole bunch. We can sleep in."

As she sighed, the pleasure of his loving kisses warming her all over, he maneuvered to the middle, commanding her full lips. "We can go dancing till two o'clock in the morning if we want. Dance till we drop. You used to like to do that, sweetheart," he finished with a whisper in her ear.

"Mmm. That sounds really nice. And I'm going to

look forward to that hot tub, too, because I'm going to miss my bathtub."

"It'll be worth it," Kyle whispered. "Trust me. I'll make sure you're pampered, loved, and pleasured every day. Anything you want, it's yours," he said as he patted her rear.

She was ready to drop her clothes on the spot, but of course, the kids were on the balcony, and she knew both of them would have to keep at least one eye on them until they got to a safer place or some supervision. But it was fun to feel him try to reel her in anyhow, knowing he wasn't really ignoring his brood. Kyle just loved tempting her. He was unabashed and generous in his affection for her and always would be.

"Are you prepared to give them a little sex education, then? Is that what you're trying to do, Kyle?" she purred.

"They're going to have to figure it out some day," he played right back to her, daring her further.

His hands slid under her shirt. She followed by finding his junk and giving him the same kind of squeeze. "Oh man, Mrs. Lansdowne, your fingers are wickedly delicious. Just what in the world am I going to do with you?"

Maggie stepped up on the tiny glass-top table to be able to lean over the railing farther. "Hold that thought, lover boy. Duty calls." She was out onto the deck in a flash, pulled down Maggie's pants, and gave her two swift spanks on her bare bottom. Kyle was right behind her.

Maggie burst into tears, scared by the jerking motion her mother made, and then dove into her mother's embrace, shivering in her love.

"Don't you ever do that again, Maggie," she cooed to the six-year-old, who had erupted into a gasping, painful cry, nearly losing full control of her body. Christy picked her up and brought her back into the room, laying her down on the bed while she sat beside her. She knew without looking Kyle was lecturing the boys, who were watching with wide eyes.

"I'm sorry, Mama. I didn't mean to—"

"It's okay now. But you know, Maggie, it could have all been over fast. You could have fallen overboard, and that would be that. No more Maggie. No more beautiful Maggie. You have to be careful, especially in places you are not familiar with. I can't always be with you everywhere all the time. You're old enough to start using your head. You're not a little girl anymore, sweetheart."

"I know. But I wanted to see the people walking onto the ship. I saw some of my friends," Maggie insisted, her gasping for breath subsiding.

"And just think what your friends would have seen if you'd have fallen. You could have just waved to them instead of putting your life in danger, Maggie."

"But they couldn't see me. I'm too short."

"That's not a good enough reason to die, sweetheart. You *know* this. Don't you, honey?" She brushed the hair from her daughter's forehead and watched her nod agreement. "All better now?" she asked, touching Maggie's cheek.

"I think so. Can I have rabbit?"

Maggie's favorite toy was a stuffed pink rabbit she'd had since a baby, which had seen great risk to life and limb anytime Brandon or Luke might want to punish it. As a matter of fact, Christy had had to replace the old one with several new versions over the years because the boys had successfully offed the favorite toy several times. It had been tossed from the car when Maggie was sleeping, thrown into the mud in their backyard, taken to the Brownlee pool and drowned more than once, and barbequed. The poor bunny toy had a horrible childhood, Christy mused. But if Maggie noticed, she made no comment about the fact that her bunny seemed to be made of Teflon or had nine lives like a cat.

She found the toy in Maggie's backpack and placed it under her chin. "There. Sabrina's needing a little comfort too."

Her daughter rolled over, hugging the bunny and very discretely tucked her thumb into her mouth.

Christy covered her with a blanket and gave her a kiss on the cheek.

Watching Kyle deal with the other two men in her life, she was grateful for his energy, how excited he was to be a father, and for every phase of their lives together. They'd shared their bit of bad news and weathered the storms of Kyle's occasional uncertain future on the Teams, the loss of one of his guys, or a divorce in their community. They shared everything, and she wouldn't want it any other way.

Little did she know that day when she went to hold her very first open house—*at the wrong address, no less*—that she'd fall for a naked guy taking a nap in the back bedroom sporting a world-class boner. He'd been ready for her then, she mused, and he was always ready for her now. All she could give him was everything she had inside. They both knew that life wasn't always fair, but for what they had today, they'd enjoy every minute. Never speaking about it between them, she knew that their love could just as easily be snuffed out, like how she'd described Maggie's lapse in judgement.

Whatever they had, it was a gift and always would be. Others weren't so lucky. It made what they did share together sweeter.

Kyle must have felt her adoring gaze on him as he turned, his blue eyes gleaming back at her, wiggling his eyebrows as he pretended to hang on every word

Brandon was telling him. She knew his attention was elsewhere. He'd always look young, with a boyish charm and energy that hid that mark of a true leader. His confidence masked all the fears she knew he had sometimes. He had that tremendous capacity to trust people, and in turn, they worked to full capacity for him. His men would do anything to save him. But they'd have to take a back seat to Christy. Christy would take the pole position every time.

He gently guided the boys back inside and whispered that they not wake Maggie up.

"You want to take them on a tour of the children's center? I was thinking I could get ready for dinner, maybe take Maggie down there on my way? I could meet you at the dining room."

"What time's the seating? We have early, right?"

"Yup. Six. And it's not fancy, but several of the ladies said they were going to dress up, so I thought I'd do my best." She smiled, a little shy about knowing he was going to make a comment that would make her blush.

He didn't disappoint.

"Honey, you could wear your flipflops and that's all, and it would be plenty fancy for me."

"Ew, Dad. That's not nice. Mom wouldn't ever go to dinner naked!" giggled Luke.

"Oh, back in the day—"

Christy was quick to cover his mouth with hers. "You have a dirty mind, but I don't care," she whispered.

Brandon began tugging on Kyle's arm. "Come on, Dad. Are we going to stay here or go downstairs? I want to see *everything!*"

"Me too!" said Luke.

And that ended Maggie's nap. "I want to go. Can I?" she said, sitting up but still clutching the bunny.

"That settles it, then. Daddy will take you all down to the center where I understand they have a very special kids' dinner all set up while we let Mommy get dressed." He winked as the kids cheered. "I'll see you downstairs then at dinner?"

"Yes, you will, Mr. Lansdowne, and probably more of me later too."

"Vera vera nice." He winked and was out the door in seconds. Then he re-opened the door and tossed Christy Maggie's rabbit.

CHAPTER 4

KYLE TOOK THE three children three levels down to the kids' center, meeting up with several of his other SEAL dads on the way. Luke and Brandon ran ahead when they saw some of their friends and disappeared behind the huge doors to the center. Maggie made it inside right after them, leaving Kyle by himself for a quick minute until he noticed Fredo approaching.

Fredo had his twins in tow, Luis and Diego, who had just turned four. His older son, Ricardo, was reluctantly straggling behind. He stopped, his hands slumped in his jeans pockets.

"I don't want to play with all the babies, Dad. I really don't. Can I stay with you?" Fredo's eight-year-old asked.

"I'm not a baby!" Diego shouted back.

"Me neither," confirmed Luis.

"I got orders from your mom all three of you are to stay here. They have a really good program for you tonight, and we'll pick you up after our dinner."

This did not make the youngster happy.

"Honest, Ricardo. That goes for you two as well. Be respectful, of everyone. Be social, friendly, and no takeaway games, okay? No fights, understood? There's going to be a bunch of other kids here, both girls and boys, and I want you to be a good representative of our family. You got that?"

Kyle was struck by how tender Fredo was with Ricardo, who was Gia's child from her previous relationship and not of his blood. The kid had grown up with lots of problems initially, but in time and long before the twins were born, he'd managed to settle down. He was doing very well in school—the first time ever, in fact.

Kyle mussed the top of the boy's head. "Brandon's looking forward to seeing you, bud. And just for your information, he feels the same way about all the younger kids and, of course, the girls."

"You gotta learn to play nice with the girls, Ricardo, or they'll get even. You know they do," advised Fredo, grabbing his son's shoulder after he opened the doors and the twins raced inside, screaming.

It was as if the twins had thrown a mud pie at him. "See? *That's* what I don't like. I'm like the oldest one, and they always want to play with my stuff, and they don't know how to use things. There aren't any older kids here because this is like Baby Central or something, Dad. I don't want to play dress-up or house or play with dolls."

"Just give it a try." Kyle wanted to be helpful, and he understood perfectly what Ricardo was going through. "We'll see if we can work something out later on. Maybe the dads can take turns with a few of you, play some basketball up top or something. I'll see if Fredo and I can arrange it. Would that help?" Kyle asked.

"Sure. And there's swimming too. We don't mind lying out by the pool."

"Grownup stuff. Watching the older girls. You know I was once your age, Ricardo," his dad whispered.

"How could I forget?" Ricardo's voice drifted off, resigned, unenthusiastic, looking as uncomfortable and bored as he could be.

"Hey, you 'dissing me?" Fredo challenged him.

Ricardo frowned and rolled his shoulder, waiting for his turn as if he was being forced to walk the plank.

Upon opening the wide yellow double doors, Kyle found a huge playroom, and in the very center of the room was a tree fort built like a Swiss Family Robinson structure with steps, ladders, poles, ropes, and slides coming from the second and third floors above. Rock music blared. A line of tricycles stood to attention in the corner, waiting to be chosen. A cottage in the corner of the room was set up as a dress-up room, stocked with hats, sequined dresses, and long, flowing wizard robes.

A miniature kitchen was fully stocked with plastic food, dishes and pans, a miniature table, chairs, refrigerator, and stove. A big screen took up an entire wall with child-sized couches and lounge chairs in clusters arranged around it.

But as impressive as the place was, Kyle was most pleased with the friendly staff, each dressed in some sort of costume. Some were animals. Others dressed in children's type clothes—little knickers, shorts with suspenders, and skirts for the girls with their ponytails, bobby socks, and saddle shoes. Everywhere Kyle looked, there were staff members around.

Through an archway that was covered with artificial tree limbs was a rain forest dotted with various jungle animals in animation. A long table with a king and queen chair at each end and other various unusually shaped and colored chairs on both sides of the table made it a perfect scene from Mad Hatter's tea party. The table overflowed with stacks of sandwiches, other finger foods, and cut up fruits. A big ice chest in the corner held soft drinks that were healthy, and a juice bar with a running faucet dispensed fresh pineapple juice.

The boys had run over to the tree house and attempted to climb the stairs. Two of the staffers stopped them and fitted them with a full-on harness and cable so that they wouldn't be harmed if they chose to or if they accidentally fell or jumped from the top. Each child had their own spotter.

Kyle looked at Fredo and shook his head. "God, I could stay here all day. I mean, if they had a climbing wall, it'd be perfect."

One of the attendants piped up, "We have one. It's over on the other side of the forest." He pointed. "We also have a small jacuzzi and several sandboxes."

Fredo was stunned. His two boys, after their initial enthusiasm, looked at all the colorful items with wide-eyed anticipation.

"You want to go play with these guys, go ride your tricycles, or do a climb?" Fredo asked.

The twins cautiously examined all the equipment, rooms, and stations, still holding hands. But Ricardo had taken up a position right next to Brandon, and the two of them were racing to scale up the tree house as fast as they could. Luke was a distant third.

As the minutes flew by, several other children and their parents entered. Kyle greeted Danny Begay with his eight-year-old son, Ali. Griffin was right behind him, but Danny held their youngest, Chester, who was only three.

"I don't think he's ready for this level of play," he said.

One of the attendant girls in the room came up and asked if she could hold Chester, and amazingly, Chester threw out his arms and let her take him.

"We have sandboxes in the other room and some Play-Doh and other things for the little ones, so don't worry they'll be supervised."

One of the other attendants had all of the parents sign in with their child's name, age, any allergies to food, as well as the text messaging app for the Center, so they could interface and let them know what time the parents would be arriving back.

Will and Gillian came with Libby Cooper, who also brought Courtney Talbot, T.J. and Shannon's daughter. Then Ginger dropped off Jasmine and Jennifer, both of them not sure they wanted to stay at first since there were so many boys present.

Kyle shook hands with his other team members and wives and greeted several other parents from the ship then jogged his way down the hall, running up the stairway to the tenth level where their room was located.

As he opened the door, he could smell Christy's floral perfume but saw no sign of Christy. He was more than disappointed he'd missed her.

After his shower and fresh shave, Kyle arrived at

the large dining room, its ceiling covered in beautiful blooming pieces of stainless steel and Venetian glass flower sculptures that twinkled. Everywhere he turned, he saw brightly colored upholstered benches, high-backed seats, and marble rotundas holding statues as if they were in a palace on the Mediterranean. Everything about the décor on the Italian registry ship was over the top.

He scanned the dining room, looking for Christy, when a waiter in a white tux approached him.

"Do you have your table number?" he asked.

"We are a large group. I can't remember the numbers. My wife and several couples should be here. We have, I think, fifty-something in all."

"Ah, the military families. Yes, we've all been anticipating your arrival."

Kyle frowned a bit, concerned that too much was known about them to begin with, but he didn't allow it to dampen his mood. He was so ready for a vacation, a few nice days of sun, and not having to cook or clean or wrangle the kids, which had been his lot in life since their return from their last deployment.

He followed the portly gentleman in the white tux until a large roped-off area loomed in front of him. Lifting the velvet separator, the waiter gestured for Kyle to make his way inside.

The room was a pleasant surprise. It was semiprivate, which appealed to him. The walls were decorated in a burgundy-colored, velvety flocked wallpaper, and the windows were rimmed in orange and turquoise neon bars. Little portholes on top let in light while the large picture windows below had built-in bench seats. Scattered throughout the room were several tables, and it was obvious that this was their room to do with what they wanted. Some of the SEALs and their wives had already started making clusters of tables, continuing to add more until finally the entire room appeared to be set up as one gigantic table with chairs all around.

"Would you look at that, Kyle. We've got ourselves a square round table," said Trace Bennett.

Kyle shook his hand and asked if Gretchen was here yet.

"On her way, I hope."

"I saw the girls downstairs. I think they were a little bit hesitant with all the boys in the room."

"Oh, don't let that fool you, Kyle. Those girls will give the guys a run for their money any day. When they get going, they're impossible to stop," assured Trace.

He saw Christy wave to him from across the way, dressed in a flowing dark blue and extremely low-cut gown that accentuated all the things he loved about her. Her hair was done up on top of her head with ringlets falling down around her shoulders. She wore the silver Trident that he had bought her for Christmas and the matching Trident earrings. They weren't as elegant as perhaps diamonds and gemstones that other men might buy their wives, but Christy wore her Tridents proudly, having earned them in every way possible except being a real SEAL.

When he approached her, giving her a kiss on the cheek, she asked, "How is it?"

"You would not believe that place. I have never seen anything so spectacular. It reminds me of something we'd see in Disneyland. Honest."

"Well, that's good. Maggie hold her own?"

"I lost her right away. She found a couple other kids she knew. I'm not good on all the names yet, but you probably know them all."

"I see those lists at night when I got to bed. Glad they seem to be having a good time."

"Maggie engaged right away. I think she's going to challenge the boys. They have it very well-staffed, and they're going to let me know by cell phone if something happens. Otherwise, we have to be back there by eight-thirty."

"So they're serving them a good dinner?"

"Well, I guess you'd call it that. Looked very healthy to me. They have a juice bar, believe it or not. Looks like they're going to have hot dogs, sandwiches, chips and salsa, cut up pieces of fruit, and chocolate milk—I mean, you name it they've got it. If they don't come home with a full tummy, they've been overly distracted by the tree fort, climbing wall, the swimming pool, the Play-Doh area, the sandboxes, and the trikes. Get this—they even hook them up to wear a harness and cable, so if they want to jump off of the top of the tree house, they can!"

"I guess it's going to take both of us to be able to pry them away, from the sounds of it. They'll probably cry all the way back to their rooms."

"I think so, Christy. I don't know how you found out about this ship, but I'm impressed with absolutely everything. It's gorgeous. And we haven't even seen the shows, tasted the food, or anything. I'm overwhelmed."

A string of waiters entered the room, and the headwaiter announced that dinner would be served as soon as at least fifty percent of the chairs were occupied, so people began taking their places, clustering together. Then the ordering began. Included in their fare was unlimited wine, champagne, and assorted soft drinks, so once the wine and champagne started flowing, the decibel level of their conversations doubled.

They were allowed servings of steak, lobster, crab, fine Italian food, and anything they liked for an entree, and they could have four or five desserts if they chose.

Kyle mused that the dining hall was adults' paradise just like the kids' center was for the children. The food was delicious, and the conversation was lively. Jokes were being told. Smack talk abounded. Introductions were made. Two of the women stood up to reveal that they were more than a little pregnant. Lizzie, Jamison's wife, introduced herself first to the group. Then Kiley, Jason's wife, introduced herself and her rather large belly. There were four nursing babies, all boys, each one held up and introduced to the group. The comment was made by Christy that there were more children on the trip than adults.

Kyle studied the faces of the men and women that helped support SEAL Team 3—the couples who dedicated their lives to service, often putting off family things to be able to serve. These couples went through tragedy and heartache and fear—always worried about coming home safely but deploying anyway. As he looked from face to face, he felt a great deal of pride at the team that had been assembled, even knowing this was only about a third of the entire SEAL Team 3.

Not all these men and women were on the first cruise some ten years ago when they traveled from Italy to South America, but the stories had abounded for years, expanding in scope and size with each telling, such that anybody who could afford to go did. If they needed help, the team pitched in to include them. He was sad more were not able to come.

Kyle's best friend was Armando Guzman, and he and his wife, Gina, were having a rough patch. Gina had been sick with two pregnancies in a row after the birth of their son, Artemis. She lost both of them. As a couple, they were struggling—though still very much in love—but Kyle worried about them constantly.

Gina was in a high stress job, being a San Diego policewoman, and there were lots of changes going on in the department, which weighed on her. Armando disclosed that he was trying to convince her to quit, but Gina was as dedicated as all the men on SEAL Team 3 and wasn't having any of it. It was something that was going to have to get resolved sooner or later.

All the same, Kyle missed his best friend and had made a point of calling him before they left for the ship.

"Why don't you just hop aboard, Armando? Not like we couldn't get you a waiver, make you an officer of the ship, perhaps. It would do you good, even if Gina can't come."

"Now is not a good time, Kyle, but thanks. I'll be thinking about you. And give a good send-off to old Gunny for me. I'll be thinking about him too."

"You got it. Be well, my friend," Kyle had signed off.

Just before their food arrived, the engines started

rumbling as the giant Italian luxury ship began leaving port. They were situated on the opposite side and couldn't see their leaving, but they watched the cityscape move past them, including familiar sites of the harbor and Coronado Island. A destroyer cruised back into port as if telling them all would be well.

The new adventure had begun!

CHAPTER 5

CHRISTY OPTED NOT to stay for the cigars out on the forward deck, like some of the wives, and instead perused the stores with Libby Cooper, her favorite shopping partner. Brandy Hudson and Shannon Talbot both came along as well, burping nursing babies. Christy asked to hold Shannon's boy, Zeus.

"Oh my God! He's a ton of bricks," she said, looking at the hulking, dark-haired, and brown-eyed little guy. "And his head is covered in black hair too! He looks just like his older brother, Magnus."

"I know," said Shannon. "I'm sure it came from T.J.'s side, because Courtney is still a carrot-top like Frankie was as a kid." Her tender smile brought a tear to Christy's eyes.

"How are Frankie's folks doing?" she asked.

"Honestly, still fighting. His sisters have been really nice, though, helping out with the kids now and then. It has made a big difference."

"Huge difference between two and three. That's when I decided not to go for four. Not that Kyle couldn't sweet talk himself into another one, but I think we're done," answered Christy, squeezing the baby's little nose. He broke out in a wide grin with sparkling dark eyes.

"Oh, look at him! What a lady killer!" said Libby, peering over Christy's shoulder.

"Do you remember those days? When ours were this little?"

"Some of the happiest of my life," Libby whispered. She drew her arm around her friend's shoulders and touched foreheads. "You were such a fantastic mom, Christy."

Christy reared her head back and wrinkled her nose. "Still am, I hope! I'm not that old!"

With the baby starting to fuss, she handed him back to Shannon.

"Okay, on to baby number two," she said, outstretching her arms as Brandy deposited Grover there. "And here we have another tank. I'm telling you, our team is having big bruising boys these days. Remember Libby when everyone was having girls?"

"Luci says, in their culture, that means there's a war brewing," said Brandy, who suddenly covered her mouth. The three other wives immediately looked down at their feet. "Oops. I shouldn't have said that," added Brandy, wincing.

Christy smiled down at the sweet face of a miniature Tucker, including the same wide ears that earned Tucker's nickname, Shrek. "No, we aren't afraid of war. We train for it. It's what we do, isn't it, little Grover? You going to grow up and be a warrior like your daddy?"

At barely six months of age, Grover was already trying to form words and spit bubbles at Christy in return and then sneezed.

She led the way, showing Grover the pretty things in the gift store. His eyes widened with the colorful scarves and sparkling crystal earrings she held up for him. Next, they wandered down the promenade with a jellybean store, an espresso coffee café that also sold baked sweets, and an ice cream store handing out coupons for free scoops of ice cream.

"Anyone else want a coffee?" asked Shannon.

"Sure, I'll have one," Christy said.

All four of them sat down and were waited on by a young barista wearing a red and white striped shirt and a black string tie. He scanned the backs of their ship cards and verified that they were on a special plan that included drinks.

"Christy, you guys did a great job picking this cruise line," said Brandy, soaking in all the color and the flash of European decoration.

"Thank you. I follow instructions well. We got a good agent. She did all the hard work after we figured out how many in our party there was going to be. That part got me tearing my hair out."

"I'd never heard of it before," Brandy added. "My dad has been on a bunch of cruises since he's re-married, but he's never tried Crown and Star Cruise Lines. I can't wait to show him the pictures I've been taking."

Libby agreed. "I'm going to try to talk my dad and mom into taking this same ship with the kids. I'm going to need a vacation to get over this vacation!"

Everyone laughed.

Christy added, "I think your folks would love it. I can see your mom having a ball, dancing, and shopping. She'd spend half her time in the spa."

"Absolutely," agreed Libby.

After the coffee, they wandered through the casino, which was going strong. "I can see T.J. spending some serious time here," mumbled Shannon.

On the other side of the casino was a theater with a variety show that had already begun. A large kettle-drum "boom" startled Grover, who began to cry, so Christy handed him back to Brandy, who immediately nursed him again.

"You'd think I'd lose weight. This kid is a voracious eater," said Brandy.

"Well, look at Tucker," chuckled Christy. "And speaking of weight, who cares? I think you look fabulous, Brandy. When I came home, I had circles under my eyes. I was black and blue. I looked like I'd been beat up. Kyle had to force me to eat. I got very thin—too thin. That's not healthy." She nodded for emphasis.

They finally made their way back toward the Children's Club, where they were amazed at the setup and talked with the helpers. The college-aged kids hailed from all over the world, speaking some ten different languages.

Christy got a text from Kyle.

We got twenty quick minutes before we get the kids. Wanna meet me in a lifeboat?

She smiled at the text.

Thought you'd forgotten.

Are you kidding? I've been thinking about nothing else these past two-plus hours. I'm on the starboard side, number 26 on Deck 5. That's right, btw.

Be right there. We're on Deck 5 now so you better be ready.

Perfect, sweetheart.

He signed off with a heart emoji.

"Well, ladies, I've been summoned to a lifeboat by some mysterious handsome stranger. I'll see you guys later on, probably back here?"

"I can take your three for a bit, if you want," offered Libby. "Just come by the stateroom when you're ready."

"Ohhh," whispered Shannon, widening her eyes. "How romantic."

"*Ciao, Bella!*" Christy said as she skipped through the yellow doors and into the main hallway leading to the front of the ship. She made her way through the casino, back through the marketplace, past the bank of double-sided elevators, through the lobby in front of two specialty restaurants, turned right, and came out into the warm breeze of the deck housing the bright orange lifeboats.

At number twenty-six, she knocked on the door, not seeing anyone inside. Behind her, she felt the hard body of her husband, who'd been lurking in the shadows. His hands found her rear and then smoothed over her belly as he lifted her onto the first step, then tucked his thighs beneath hers and lifted her to the second step. Holding her body in a sitting position against him, he opened the door with his right hand and, with his left, pushed it wide for her to climb inside.

She slid onto the smooth plastic bench. Kyle lay down several life vests and some blankets, adjusting them so her backside was protected. He watched her writhe in front of him as he allowed her to unbutton his shirt. Her toes found his hardness as he dropped his trousers to his knees, leaned over her, removed her panties, and, in one thrust, was deep inside her.

She decided not to tell him they had more time. She pretended she needed more coaxing to become aroused, but she touched him often, making sure he knew she was into it. He helped lift her dress over her head, and he pushed the straps on her new navy-blue bra over her shoulders to drape on her arm. He buried his head in her chest as she tilted her head back, adjusting her pelvis to receive him deeper still.

He pulled her up on top of him as he twisted, begging her to ride him, rubbing the sides of her thighs all the way to her toes as she lifted and ground down on him several times, each time feeling his length and girth expand until she could hardly breathe. She was so on the edge. She tried to hold back for fear of bursting, but his insistent push sparked her long rolling orgasm that turned her body into a furnace of desire. As he pressed deeper, her spasms overtook her. He pulled her legs up over his shoulders, impaling her on his cock, holding her ass with both hands, pressing deep until she saw stars.

Christy gasped, frozen in time, the fuse now lit began to burn, taking him away with her. For several long seconds, he held himself against her pulsating cervix until he began to spill. With great care and tenderness, they kissed silently, each drawing the magic from the other, their tongues exploring deep as she melted in his arms.

Out of breath and soaking in his man-scent, she smiled with satisfaction.

"Was it worth it? I told you it would be," he whispered.

She gently rocked against him, answering him with her kisses and unwilling to let him go. She bended one knee back, leveraging herself to ride him up and down again, luxuriating in the intimacy of the moment and hearing the sounds of their lovemaking echoing inside the little boat. As his member grew, she slipped off his lap and put him in her mouth then pulled him deep down her throat, setting up the beginning of round two.

CHAPTER 6

THE NEXT DAY, several families gathered in the cafeteria section of the top deck. They enjoyed sandwiches while allowing the kids to go back for thirds and fourths of the frozen yogurt, since the enormous machine never seemed to empty.

Kyle and Christy were laughing about the fact that Brandon and Ali, who was Danny Begay's adopted Iraqi son, had formed a special bond, and since both boys were extremely athletic and wiry, they challenged each other to everything they could master in the playroom—much to the chagrin of Luke, who was used to playing with his older brother, and tried competitively to catch up to him. Brandon and Ali played basketball together. They rappelled down the tree house in the center of the room.

But with the two boys forming this fast friendship, Luke had been left out in the cold and really didn't like being relegated to the company of some of the girls. He was waiting for Ali and Brandon to finish their turns on the frozen yogurt machine before he stepped forward a little too soon and caught an elbow in his upper cheek, right below his eye. Immediately the gash started spewing blood, and several of the girls began to scream. The boys tried to grab wads of napkins to stop the bleeding, but it was only a matter of a few seconds before Cooper, T.J., and Kyle came running to Luke's rescue.

"It's going to need a couple of stitches, Kyle," said Cooper. "I got some in my medic pack, but not sure I have enough gauze, because he's going to have to be switched out every few hours. I got the antibiotics, though, and if he needs a shot, I can give him one."

At the sound of the word shot, Luke's eyes got to the size of tangerines. He didn't say a word, but Kyle could feel his little body shaking from the anticipation of the pain of a needle in his arm or, worse, perhaps next to his eye, which no doubt scared him to death.

Kyle nodded and got down on his knees to speak to his son. "Luke, I'm afraid you're going to have to go with Cooper here, and he's going to fix you up. It's not a bad cut, but if we don't stitch it up, it might get infected or start to gap later on. And you don't want to have a big old scar right under your eye, do you?"

"No, Daddy. But will it hurt?"

"I think it will, but just a little." Kyle decided the

best policy was to be completely honest with his son.

Cooper joined Kyle, kneeling in front of the boy. "I'm real careful, Luke. In fact, sometimes people ask me when I'm going to give them a shot, and I've already done it. So I'll be as gentle as I can be, okay?"

Luke's lower lip curled outward, as his body continued shaking, but he nodded his head, indicating he understood Cooper's comment.

Kyle gave a report to Christy back at their table and let her know that he was going to follow Luke to Libby and Cooper's room so he could get the attention he needed.

"They have a doctor on board, Kyle. What about letting him take a look at it?" she asked.

Kyle shook his head vehemently, adding, "No, I'd let anybody but the ship's doctor take a look at him. These guys aren't necessarily fully licensed, I hear. I'd trust my life with Coop, and I think I'd rather Luke be seen by him."

Several at the table agreed, encouraging that decision. Christy finally said yes. "Can I see him first?"

"Sure thing." He motioned for Luke to come over and present his battle wound to his mother. She removed the napkins, not quite getting to the open wound, and upon seeing blood starting to gush again, she held the tissues over it and asked Luke to hold it in place. "Put some pressure on it, okay, sweetie?"

"Yes, Mom."

The three of them made their way through the dining hall and the lobby area then took an elevator downstairs to the tenth deck. Cooper positioned Luke on his bed, unzipping his black medic bag. He washed his hands with a special solution he had in a squeeze bottle. Then he used a fresh towel to dry his hands and asked Kyle to get another hand towel wet so he could use it to mop up the mess. "And wash your hands, Kyle."

"Sure thing."

Very carefully, Cooper removed the tissues and held his hand out for the damp towel dripping in Kyle's hand. Before he applied it, he gave it back to Kyle. "This is way too wet. Wring it out first, please, okay?"

Kyle's hands were shaking even though this wasn't the type of wound or battle scar he was used to seeing. He'd seen guys lose limbs, eyes, or take a bullet to the gut, and this had no comparison to those wounds. But this was Luke, his youngest, his son.

Cooper dabbed the area and pointed out the straight line of the gash to Kyle. "It's going to be real easy to fix this. I don't think it'll even leave a scar."

Kyle noticed the redness and puffiness that had already begun to develop around the wound and the fact that the blood was beginning to coagulate. "You're doing real good, Luke. I'm very proud of you."

"Do I have to have a shot now?"

"I don't think so, but if you hold very, very still, I'm going to put some numbing cream on it, and we're going to see if that's enough. And you tell me if it stings, and if it does, I'll give you that shot, okay?"

Kyle thought Cooper's bedside manner was perfect for Luke. His son was no doubt going to do everything he could to avoid the shot, even putting up with having his flesh stitched together, and he knew that would hurt. He was extremely proud of him.

With a tiny needle and thread, Cooper's delicate fingers placed five stitches on his cheekbone, frequently having to wipe away Luke's brave tears, reapply some of the numbing cream, and then add some antibiotics. He looked up at Kyle and asked a question, "Has he had all his shots, like tetanus and all that? I think he's supposed to have if he's gone to school, right?"

"Yes, yes, he's had everything. I'm sure of it."

He peered at Luke square in the eyes. The big sandy-haired SEAL rubbed his fingers through Luke's hair, roughing it up a bit, and told him, "You're a little trooper, Luke. Very, very brave. You know, I have stitched some guys up that had gashes smaller than this one, and sometimes they cry, and—"

Kyle interrupted, finishing Cooper's sentence.

"And we had a couple really big guys that fainted at the sight of their own blood. Can you believe that, Luke?"

Luke was heartened by the stories, giggled slightly, and showed that his mood was back on track. Kyle imagined that he'd be telling stories of how blood covered everything on the bed, he had a great big scar on his face, and maybe would have to wear an eye patch. Kyle knew that Luke was prone to exaggeration, especially if he was trying to impress the other children, like Ali and Brandon.

"Now I'm going to put a big bandage on this here stitching, so you don't get it dirty, okay?" Cooper was very calm as he removed the gauze pad from his kit and taped it down. It was in an odd spot, and Kyle knew it would have to be re-dressed more than once or twice a day.

"Luke, you need to take really good care of that, okay? You need to keep it clean, and no roughhousing for a couple of days, okay?"

Little Luke looked up at his dad with his eyes filled with pain. "But I love jumping down off the tree fort. Can I do that, Dad?"

"I want you to sit the rest of the day out, and we'll see how you are tomorrow, okay?"

Luke nodded. His hands were crossed over his thighs.

Cooper pointed out a small bruise and bump on

Luke's forearm. "What the hell is that, Luke?"

"Oh, it's nothing. I just tripped a little bit. The fall hurt my hand, but it's getting better."

Kyle examined the bump and the bruise. He let Cooper hold his son's elbow and wrist between his two hands and gently try to bend it down, but Luke immediately objected and shouted that it hurt.

"Kyle, this should be X-rayed. I think there's a chance it's a sprain, a bad sprain, or he might have broken it." Cooper looked back at him with a long, sad face.

"Come on, sport. I'm going to take you downstairs. Let's see if they've got a real doctor or a veterinarian," Kyle barked. "We need the doc's fancy machine today."

As Kyle walked away with his son, he could hear Cooper laughing in the background. "Is that your way of telling me I did okay?"

Kyle turned around and yelled back at his friend, "Yup. I think you'll make a fine doctor someday, Special Operator Cooper. Who knows, maybe you could get a passage on one of these ships, and you and Libby could sail the ocean blue in luxury."

Luke was trying to convince Kyle that the bruise on his arm and the pain he was feeling was really nothing to worry about. And he said over and over again that it was just his own dumb mistake for falling and that no one was responsible for it. That presented a red flag to

Kyle, and he knew exactly the two boys he was going to question after they had their visit to the doctor.

Since they were due to arrive at their first port, only to take on food and supplies, as well as alternating crew, the door to the cargo area was wide open to the sea. Men stood balanced on the lip of the doorway, inhaling the wind and watching the land pass by them. The crew was a combination of young men from all over the world, but the bulk of the population was either Caribbean or Korean. Kyle didn't know why that was the case, since this was an Italian cruise line, but he figured it probably had to do with the cost of labor.

Large dollies were wheeled out toward the opening and lined up, about eight deep. Three men maneuvered these huge dollies, as well as someone deep inside the bowels of the ship running a small forklift, moving pallets from one area to another. There were a lot of bodies working in close proximity, but it was orderly, and since Kyle couldn't understand a word of Korean or the Pidgeon Caribbean dialects that were spoken, he focused on what the men were doing rather than what they were saying.

He saw the picture of the white cross on a red dot and proceeded down the hallway in the direction of the arrow that was placed underneath it.

The door to the doctor's office was open, revealing an exam table and a desk tucked into the corner. With his back to the doorway, an older gentleman with graying curly hair was hunched over the desk, writing a report.

"Excuse me, sir. I'm looking for the ship's doctor," asked Kyle.

The man turned around in his wheeled chair, smiled at little Luke, looked up at Kyle, and then stood, extending his hand. "So are you the patient or is this little guy here the patient?" He was quite obviously Italian, and his English was almost unintelligible. "Excuse me, but I am Dr. Bonelli, at your service, sir." The doctor gently bowed, tucking his heels together with a dash of drama.

"Well, I'm Kyle, and this is my son Luke."

"So what seems to be the problem?" Dr. Bonelli asked.

"Well, it's his right forearm, right here." Kyle gently extended Luke's arm to show him the spot he wanted examined. "I believe you have an X-ray machine, isn't that right?"

"You would be correct, sir. And as a matter of fact, we often use it for the cargo, not usually for patients. But we have it, it's a small portable machine, but I think we will be able to take a look and see if the bones are broken."

Within twenty minutes, he was given the news that Luke had indeed broken one of the bones in his forearm. Dr. Bonelli fitted him with a splint and suggested that, on their first shore excursion, they try to find a doctor in town who could put a cast on it. "But it's not an ugly green stick break. It's pretty typical for a child's fracture. It could be that just immobilizing it would be fine."

Kyle asked if he could keep the X-rays and show them to his buddy, who he said had medical training.

"*Si, si, si.* I will put it in an envelope for you. No problem."

He indicated that there would be a fee added to his cabin charge, Kyle signed the paperwork, and the two of them left. Luke grasped a large brown envelope containing two X-rays of his arm.

As they retreated down the hallway, headed to the elevators, Kyle saw through an open doorway that two very young girls were tied to a bed frame, gagged, and crying. He held up just long enough to consider poking his head inside to find out what was going on when a pockmarked face completely obliterated the crack in the doorway. "You mind your goddamn business, sailor."

Kyle slipped Luke behind him, hoping that the nasty face staring back at him wouldn't notice, but it was too late.

"Is everything all right there?" Kyle asked.

The gentleman opened the door wide, and Kyle

stepped slightly inside, examining both girls from a distance. "Are you okay?" he asked them. But immediately, he saw that the girls probably didn't speak English.

On cue, both of the young girls nodded their heads furiously. They tried to say something under their gag, probably to argue that they were in no danger. But they looked scared. Their eyes were red from crying, and one of them had a bruise and swelling beneath her left eye.

"You see? They are fine. Now butt out of my business. This is entirely consensual." The nasty deckhand slammed the door, almost hitting Kyle in the nose.

Kyle grabbed Luke's hand and ushered him down the hallway quickly.

"Daddy! That was a bad man. I just know those girls aren't happy. I think he's being mean to them."

Kyle looked down at his son, knelt in front of him, and gave him a hug. "That's right, Luke. And your dad's going to ask about it, too. I think they did need help. But I have to go through channels here. This isn't my team. This isn't my boat."

CHAPTER 7

C HRISTY WAS SITTING with several of her girlfriends out by the family pool, taking advantage of a little bit of the shade of an overhang for the deck above. It was a warm cloudless day, and it had been weeks since she'd taken the time to lie out in her bathing suit, slather suntan lotion on, put her sunglasses on, and read a romance novel. So today, in between the banter of conversation between all the ladies, she took full advantage of it indulging herself 100%.

Of course, the steady stream of waiters who brought strawberry margaritas and other special tropical drinks helped. Some were decorated with long straws and umbrellas, others with potted parrots and extra cherries and fruit slices in them. Christy was careful to stick to just two spirits. From past experience, she knew she couldn't hold her liquor if she blended more than that. So wine was out for dinner tonight.

She looked up in time to see her handsome husband walk across the deck by the pool with little Luke in tow. It wasn't lost on her all the comments and stares several of the ladies not with their SEAL teams gave him. His handsome physique, his singleness of purpose, and the way he made a beeline straight for her with his arm on his young son's shoulder made him stand out. And then she recognized that Luke had a splint on his arm.

She put her book down, took a sip of her drink, and set it beside her, getting ready for the news.

As Kyle passed a large table of middle-aged ladies playing Gin Rummy, he got some whistles and catcalls, and she could tell by the way he rolled his eyes that it annoyed him. It would have been funny if it weren't for the fact that she was concerned about Luke's prognosis.

"Hi there, sailor. So what's up with the doctor?"

"I broke it, Mom." Luke held out his arm showing her the splint and the layers of bandage wrapped around it.

"Is it a bad break, Kyle?"

Kyle shook his head. "We're lucky it was a clean break, more of a hairline fracture. It's going to heal up really fast. He's young and healthy. Our biggest problem probably is going to be keeping his cheekbone sterile and making sure he doesn't go jumping in the water with it. It means probably no swimming this trip."

Luke knew this already, but hearing it for the first time, Christy could see it finally registered. He looked down at his toes and frowned.

"Oh, I'm sorry, sweetheart. Well, I guess that means you'll be spending a little more time with us then."

Several of the other wives smiled. Shannon, who was burping the baby, said, "I don't mind that at all. I always like to have a handsome young man at my side."

"The main thing is, we just want you to get better, and we don't want any problems down the road." Kyle looked at Christy sternly. "We'll have to X-ray it in a couple of days and see how it's healing. The doc said maybe we should put a cast on it. I'm waiting to find Coop. Have you seen him?"

"No, I haven't. Libby's not here, either. So perhaps—"

Several of the ladies laughed, and there was some guessing and discussion about where the two of them could be holed up.

"I just am not sure whether we should take him to the village when we dock, since I'm not really confident in this doctor. I'd probably feel even less confident with people in Baja, and I don't think we want to put a cast on it because it will interfere with the healing, or so I've been told. We've got real good weather and lots of heat.

I just think he's going to be better off leaving it a little bit open as long as it's stabilized." Kyle gave her a quick smile and continued searching the deck for signs of Cooper.

"Well, sweetheart, do you feel like having something to eat or do you want something to drink?" Christy asked.

"Can I have one of those drinks with all the cherries in it, the fizzy drink that has all that sweet cherry juice or something?" Luke asked.

"I can bring that right up, ma'am. Of course, you want it non-alcoholic, I presume." One of the waiters waited for Christy's acknowledgement, turned on his heel, and headed back to the bar.

Christy patted the chaise lounge and asked Luke to sit down next to her.

Kyle cocked his head so he could get a look at Zeus, who was resting over Shannon shoulder. "So tell me, Shannon, where the hell did you get the name Zeus for him?"

Christy piped up. "Kyle, that's not very nice."

"Well, you know me. I call 'em like I see 'em. Not that Zeus isn't an apt description of him. He's probably going to be as big or bigger than T.J., but I was just curious. You guys have ancestors who are Greek gods?"

Shannon laughed, holding the baby up so Kyle

could take a look at his face. "Who would you guess came up with this naming idea?"

"I'm not surprised. In fact, I probably could have answered my own question," said Kyle. "I mean, when you have an older brother named Magnus, I guess you could say Zeus kind of fits in there."

"And then, of course, there's Courtney," said Shannon. "But that's a name Frankie picked out."

"So where is the old man? I mean, there's all you beautiful ladies sitting here. I'm surprised the guys aren't keeping watch." Kyle had his hands on his hips. "What do you think, Luke? Should we go find Uncle T.J.?"

Shannon suggested that he go up one deck and to the rear and check out the basketball courts. Kyle and Luke left before the boy could get his special drink.

Ginger and her two daughters got out of the pool, dried off, and sat down on lounge pillows near Christy.

"So what do you think of the trip so far?" she asked the girls.

Clover, who was almost ready to complete high school and who had grown nearly six inches in the past year, smiled wide. That's when Christy realized she'd gotten her braces off.

"Your teeth look beautiful, Clover. Look at how you're filling in. You're going to be a beauty, just like your mama." The reaction was swift. Clover's face became bright red. Angela, her younger sister, mentioned discreetly that Clover had brought brand new underwear on the cruise.

"Oh my!" said Christy.

Gretchen shook her head and put her hand over her eyes. "Angela, we talked about this. Remember?"

"But Christy used to work in an underwear store in San Francisco, and she knows all about fancy underwear. Don't you, Christy?"

"I can see I need to be a little more careful about my discussions when I forget that little ears are listening." Christy reflected on those days, working for the little French shop owner with all the specialty bras and panties and the wealthy clients who bought them for their wives and girlfriends. It's what she had done before she moved down to San Diego and before she met Kyle.

How her life had changed.

Lizzie had been wading in the toddler pool with Sarah. Her pregnancy was causing her ankles to swell a bit. She dried off and wrapped a towel around Sarah, announcing, "I think that's going to do it for me in the sun today. I'm going to take Sarah back for nap, maybe catch one myself. I just can't take the sun and the heat anymore."

"We'll see you at dinner, then?" said Christy.

"Hope so. We'll play it by ear. I'm not feeling well.

A little dizzy."

As the two of them made their way toward the elevators, Gretchen leaned closer to Christy and whispered, "She's a cutie. What a love story those two have, don't they?"

"I'd say you have one of your own, Gretchen. I remember that trip to Hawaii. Trace didn't waste any time once he spotted you."

"Jameson's a lucky man. They make the best-looking couple."

Shannon ended the conversation with, "I think we're all pretty damn lucky. Now that's my cue. I'm going to take Zeus inside, out of the heat. I think I could use a nap as well."

Kyle and T.J. approached the ladies. He knelt over and gave Christy a kiss on her cheek, whispering, "T.J. and I are going to go downstairs and talk to the doctor for a couple of minutes. I have some questions. I never could find Coop."

"What about?" she asked.

"Just some stuff I saw downstairs that doesn't make a whole lot of sense. And I kind of wanted a second opinion on it." Kyle shrugged his shoulders, which told Christy that was going to be the end of it. But she attempted further explanation anyway.

"Is everything okay?"

"Everything is perfect," he whispered to her lips.

"Right as rain."

"Daddy, can I come?"

"I think you better stay here, Luke. This is just something Daddy's got to go do." He winked at Christy, but his obvious attempt to try to look casual set off all kinds of alarms in her head. He was up to something, and whatever it was, it wasn't good.

CHAPTER 8

KYLE AND T.J. entered the Deck 2 area, which was the loading and unloading dock, as well as the medical office. As the ship came closer to land, the activity increased. All of a sudden, hands descended upon the area like somebody had stepped on an anthill. People walked back and forth with carts and dollies. Crews of men packed up boxes, wrapped containers full of trash, and lined up receiving pallets for what was to come onboard. It was probably a very dangerous time for any of the paying passengers to be present.

T.J. was muttering under his breath. "God, I hope I don't get run over by a forklift. I've never seen a ship so busy."

"Yeah, me neither. They are definitely a well-oiled crew. Makes you appreciate all the things that we get onboard, not knowing all of the people it takes to provide those things. I really had no idea, since the only time I've been down here, we've been either cruising or getting ready for a couple of hours on shore as a passenger."

Eventually, they sneaked through the lines and groups of men carrying supplies, wheeling dollies, and stripping packaging from containers for distribution. Most of the cargo area looked like the top of a container ship, with items on pallets, wrapped in plastic, labeled, and inventoried. Kyle figured that every day they had instructions which pallet to unwrap and which supplies to deliver where, since it would be impossible to store everything they needed upstairs where the passengers were. Supplies were pulled out on a strict schedule, he guessed.

The medical office door was closed and locked. Kyle noticed the sign indicating that office hours were not going to be until later this evening when they were back at sea.

An engineering officer with a walkie-talkie confronted the two SEALs. "You guys shouldn't be down here. It's off limits to passengers. You want to get yourself killed? Are you idiots? I want you out of here right away. You don't belong." His slight Italian accent was extremely stern and serious. Kyle knew there was a tremendous liability should they be hurt that was leading to the officer's stress level.

He wondered about approaching him with his concerns about the girls and started, "Sir, I'd like to contact the ship's doctor, if I may. I was down here earlier with my son, and I'd like to address a couple of things that I observed."

"Like what?"

"I'd like a private word with him. That's all."

Looking closer, Kyle could see the unfriendly eyes of someone who was going to give him trouble, and he really didn't want to press anything, especially since he had no real firsthand knowledge of the situation. He needed more information before he'd stick his neck out too far. It wasn't cowardice. It was just being smart. And he recognized in the engineering chief that his goal was to make sure the orderly transfer of goods occurred without any other distraction.

"Then if it's a medical issue, you'll have to come back. I take it there's no emergency?" The beefy officer checked over both Kyle and T.J.s exposed tats on their arms and the size of their arms, as well, then peered closer, extending his chin outward, as he whispered, "I don't think this is the time."

His lack of blink and his apparent disregard for his own safety helped Kyle to understand that he was perhaps a very dangerous man.

"I beg your pardon, sir. I will attend to the doctor later on then. I'm sorry I bothered you." Kyle didn't back up, instead waiting for the engineer to have his fill, as he was still sizing up their physique, their muscles, their arms and tats, what they wore, and the shortness of their hair. Kyle figured he had fairly good intuition that they were paramilitary of some kind. The fact that this gentleman was familiar with military and wasn't afraid meant that he had some training as well.

The engineer heard something on his walkie-talkie, which gave him an out. He turned to the side, stepped a little farther into the landing area, and spoke into the walkie-talkie in Italian. As he finished up, he nodded to Kyle and T.J. and gave them a wave, dismissing them.

Kyle could feel T.J.'s anger boiling. "I get that it's an inconvenient time, but I don't understand why he would treat paying customers like he just did. Makes me suspicious. You think he might have something to hide?"

"You mean it's not all about liability to the cruise line?"

"Yup."

"I'm going to walk past the stateroom, and I'm going to bump your arm when I come close to it. Just give it a good whack, and let's see if we can stir up some chickens. You okay with that? What I'd like you to do is bang on the door as we walk past, only if Mr. Engineer here isn't watching us."

Kyle heard T.J. grunt, and as they came to the doorway where the girls had been, he gave T.J. an elbow jab to the ribs. T.J. turned to look behind him then made his hand into a fist and banged on the door one hard time, as if he was angry at something, while they continued walking. Both of them listened for the sound of a door being opened, but there was none.

In front of the elevators, Kyle dialed a phone number.

"What the hell are you doing, Kyle?" T.J. asked.

"I'm dialing the phone number on the door, trying to get the doc." He put the phone to his ear when he heard a male voice answer.

"This is Dr. Bonelli. What can I do for you?"

"Doctor, this is Kyle Lansdown, and you treated my little boy earlier today, just about an hour ago?"

"*Si si,* is there some problem with him now?"

"No, sir, but I have a question for you, if you don't mind. My wife has asked me to come speak to you about a couple of items. Are you available right now?"

"Well, I am going to be working out at the spa. I have an appointment there in about an hour, but I have some time now. Would you like to meet me at the coffee bar perhaps?"

"Perfect. Will be there in five minutes."

"Well, it will be longer than that for me. I've just taken a shower. I will be there as soon as I can. Order yourself some espresso and a pastry if you like. I'll be there shortly."

The two SEALs elected to run upstairs three decks,

since they had not had their regular fill of exercise. Once at the lobby level, they walked past several shops and cafes on the Grand Promenade and found the little coffee house. The smell of fresh roasted espresso was tantalizing. At home, Kyle would have had three or four by now, but today, this was going to be his first.

T.J. found a table in a corner while Kyle ordered their coffees. Both of them tried a chocolate croissant as well.

Approximately ten minutes later, Dr. Bonelli arrived, waving to them in the corner. He ordered a coffee and pastry and came to join them.

"So what's this all about?" Dr. Bonelli asked as he pulled out a chair and sat at the marble top table.

"Well, my son is fine, and I thank you for that, although he's not happy about not being able to swim. But that's not why I'm here, Doctor. On my way back, Luke and I saw something that disturbed me greatly."

"And what would that be?" the doctor asked, examining his coffee with a frown.

"I saw two very young women tied up against a bed frame and gagged. They didn't look like they were having a good time. In fact, they looked like they had been abused. Now, I have no authority here, and I'm coming to you first, but this type of situation, and I'm sure you're aware of this, is not acceptable. This is a family ship, and even if this is consensual behavior, which I don't think it was, I don't want my children to see anything like this. And Luke did. And that's why I'm here, asking you these hard questions, Dr. Bonelli."

"I see. Well, Mister, what was your name again?"

"I'm Kyle, and this is T.J."

"So, Kyle, I am not the boss of the men here. I am on very tender hooks with no power or no ability to say yay or nay to anything. These men do not work for me. I have absolutely nothing to do with any of it. This would be the purview of one of the officers, and if what you say is true, and I certainly have no reason to doubt you, then I will present it to them myself. I'm sure you can appreciate that the officers on board this vessel will take every opportunity to do a full investigation."

Kyle could see Dr. Bonelli's hesitation in meeting his gaze directly, indicating a certain amount of deception. Maybe it was a white lie or maybe it was some kind of fear that was making him incapable of confronting the situation.

T.J. leaned on his elbows and ask the doctor a question. "So are these guys who work here contracted with the cruise line, private contractors, or freelancers?"

Dr. Bonelli shrugged his shoulders. "I have no idea, gentlemen. This has nothing to do with me. I have no knowledge of how any of this operates. All I'm responsible for is the health and safety of the patients who come to see me."

"So what if one of these girls was to come to you, and you could see that she'd been misused, had a black eye, her wrists were red from being bound, and she'd been crying or upset. As a doctor, wouldn't you investigate?"

Dr. Bonelli cocked his head from side to side then back and forth several times, deep in thought. "What is abuse? What is consensual? And who am I to make any sorts of accusations? You see, Kyle, I have no authority and no power to question anything. I would treat the woman. I would ask her if she needed to speak to someone else, like perhaps a counselor. We have two priests on board, and we have other staff who can counsel people. I would treat any wounds, and I would suggest that she take her situation further. That's all I can do. I have no right to accuse anybody on the ship's staff of anything. Especially since I didn't see what occurred."

"Dr. Bonelli, are you licensed in the United States of America?" Kyle asked.

"No, I am licensed in the Dominican Republic right now."

"In the brochure that we obtained about this cruise, it said there is a U.S. licensed physician on staff here. Apparently, that was untrue?"

Dr. Bonelli wanted to scan the room, Kyle could see. He briefly looked to his right and left, no doubt seaching for a senior crew member. When he didn't see one, he leaned into the table and whispered, "My medical license in the State of Florida has expired. But I did practice in Florida for nearly a decade. I am waiting for it to be re-instated. It was simply a lapse on my part." He placed his hand on his chest right below his neck and then added "Probably at the time the brochures were printed, I was licensed in the United States. So you can see it is a technical issue. Something I regret. But it's my fault."

Kyle noted that Dr. Bonelli, trying to be very charming and casual about the situation, was beginning to resemble a caged animal. The top of his forehead perspired, as well as underneath his nose along his upper lip. He gulped down half a glass of water and then sat back in his chair with an obvious sigh, giving in to the stress.

"We're not here to cause any problems with you, Doctor. We have no quarrel with you or how you treated my son. Our only interest is to make sure that the ship is not carrying human bondage and that all the international rules about human trafficking and slavery are being observed. But you should understand, Dr. Bonelli, both T.J. and I have seen these things, mostly in the countries of origin where these women have been stolen from their families, from their loved ones, from their mothers and fathers. It is something that we've tried very hard in our capacity working for the United States government to eliminate, and we are charged to report it if we see it. But we have no quarrel with you. I'm looking for a reasonable answer. I'm expecting that you tell the senior officers here, and if you do not, I promise you, Dr. Bonelli, I will."

CHAPTER 9

CHRISTY WAS GETTING her three children ready for dinner. Since it was to be Italian night, they had decided to have a family dinner in their private dining room. It wasn't formal, but the kids were not to show up in flip-flops and bathing suits.

One by one, Luke, Brandon, and Maggie allowed her to dress them and get their hair straight, and she put something on the TV that she hoped would satisfy them, a program about animals in the rainforest. She propped them up on the bed, all three of them in a row, and jumped into the shower. She knew that Kyle would be coming in soon, and she wanted to be ready when he got here.

She started to dress inside the tiny bathroom and was frustrated as her elbows hit the mirror then hit the side of the shower, but she didn't want to dress in front of the children so stuck it out long enough to at least get her underwear and her slip on. Then she came out into the bedroom and finished dressing.

Kyle walked through the door, and the kids lit up with greetings for him. He went over to examine Luke's arm and check his patch, determining that he would have to get a new bandage soon.

"I checked it out, too. I took it off before he took his shower, Kyle. It looks okay to me, but I think we'll need new tape," Christy said to him.

Kyle had pulled the tape off and was examining the stitches. "Yeah, he's going to be just fine I think, but you're right. We need to change this bandage and get more tape on him." He stood up straight and gave her a smile, letting her know he liked the way she looked in her slip.

"So what did you and T.J. do, if I can ask?"

Kyle sat on the end of the bed and stripped off his shirt and shorts, kicking off his canvas slip-on shoes as well. He inhaled deeply. Then, with his elbows leaning on his knees, he began, "T.J. and I went downstairs to talk to the doc. Boy, there's a lot going on down there. I guess this little refueling station is a big deal for them. So there were workers all over the place. It was a mess but an organized mess."

"Was the doctor gone?" she asked.

"Yeah. I called him, and T.J. and I met him up in the cafe. Very interesting fellow."

Christy slipped on her slacks and top. She put her

hair up, and then put her Trident necklace and earrings on.

"And?"

Kyle scanned the three kids sitting on the bed. "Perhaps in a little bit? I think I'd like to talk to you in private about it."

"Fine."

Christy picked up Gunny's urn and sat next to the kids on the bed. "I think we're all ready when you are Kyle. Or do you want us to meet you at the dining room?"

"No, I'll just be five minutes here. Hang on."

As she sat, she twisted the urn in her hands, looking at the tarnished sides of it and thinking about where it had been and why, after so many years, it had been returned to her. It was to be their evening together before they went up top and released Gunny's ashes to the ocean. She hoped that the new sendoff would inspire the team and the families to a new level of commitment and demonstrate to the children in their family their honor and respect for someone who had fallen before them.

Growing up, Christy had a somewhat jaded opinion of death, and she never liked the idea of celebrating someone's life after they were gone. It had been difficult to say goodbye to her mother, as well as Madame M., the owner of the lingerie shop in San Francisco, and she had long conversations with Tom Bergeron about the death of his wife. They always skirted the issue of that permanent disengagement, and whenever Kyle left, for deployment, they never said goodbye, which was something that many others in their group adhered to as well. It was always more important to welcome them home than to say goodbye.

So this ceremony tonight was weighing a little heavily on her chest. And she was curious what new things Kyle had discovered. He was not the type of man who would just keep quiet about something that was a bother to himself or others. And that often made it so that he was inserted in other people's business, and it opened him up to danger from time-to-time. But that's the way he was, and that's the man she married. And she would have to wait for him to explain it fully to her.

Kyle exited the tiny bathroom in his underwear, quickly dressed, placed some aftershave on his fresh cheeks, and called it done.

They escorted their little family upstairs to the dining hall, Christy holding Kyle's hand with her left while she gripped Gunny's urn in her right.

The children, of course, had their favorites and, within reason, were accommodated. Everyone sat after the orders were taken, and Kyle clicked on his water bottle to bring everyone to attention.

"Well, this was an excuse to have a good time together as a family, because our warrior community needs to celebrate family, the people we work for," he gestured to the audience in front of him while several chuckled.

"And we wanted to do this right. We just didn't think it was honorable to toss Gunny away, our intention had always been to have a ceremony and send him off the way we had planned. But as you know, that cruise was anything but normal. Life happened, and Gunny was lost. We thought he was floating out there already, and then two months ago, he showed up again."

The chuckling began as Kyle held Gunny's urn so all could see.

"So now, it's incumbent upon us to give him that sendoff that he deserves. And I'm sure all of you know that Gunny's son, Sanouk, is here to help with the honors. And accompanying Sanouk is our old former handler, Master Chief Timmons, who has taken on the new role in Sanouk's life as his stepfather. Many of you weren't around when Timmons was our liaison. And he did a fine job for us, kept us out of trouble, and helped us make some very important decisions, even went to bat for us on occasion. It was an honor to serve with him, and we wanted him to be here, as well, not only because we wanted to show him respect, but because he knew Gunny so well and married Gunny's wife."

Again, the crowd chuckled.

Even among the older generations, the retired guys, when a warrior left a widow, someone would step in to take care of her. Timmons, recently divorced and very unhappy in his marriage, found love and solace with the beautiful Thai woman who had borne Gunny's child years ago.

"So I give you Sanouk and Master Chief Timmons."

The crowd clapped and whistled as the young, gangly son of their favorite Marine Gunnery Sergeant stood up, all twenty-seven years of him, obviously embarrassed but deeply moved. Next to him, with his arm around his stepson, was Timmons.

"I think you should talk first," Sanouk said to Timmons. Christy could tell a good case of nerves half a football field away. Sanouk was petrified of speaking to this group.

Timmons removed his arm, distanced himself slightly from Sanouk, and cleared his throat. "All right, here we go. I've been trying to rehearse something for days now, and Amornpan, Sanouk's mother, has given me strict instructions on what I am to say and what I am not to say. So on pain of death, let's all hope I say the right thing."

The crowd laughed. A few clapped.

"Gunny was one of those guys that would give anything he had to help a fellow warrior in need. He was a surrogate father to some. He was a brother that perhaps we never had or had lost," he said with his hand over his heart. "He was a father, and we figure he had at least twelve children, but it was the greatest joy of his life to finally meet one of them."

Again, chuckles rippled through the room.

"He was fond of saying that he loved getting married and he loved having children. It was the staying married and sticking around that he failed at. He also made a point to tell anybody who would listen that he didn't believe in divorce, so we believe that he had at least five wives."

He turned to Sanouk, addressing him. "He told me on several occasions that Sanouk's mother, Amornpan, was the love of his life. They got married in the jungle in Thailand, and Gunny intended to bring her to the United States. However, she became pregnant, and Gunny never knew this. The family urged her to stay in Thailand. Old Gunner thought she'd changed her mind, so after initially trying, he gave up on the idea of bringing her to America."

"So you can imagine how he felt when he found out that he had a son and a wife who still loved him. Your mother, Sanouk, came and took care of Gunny in his last days. It is something that all of us should hope for, that we have someone so loving and caring to carry out our final wishes."

Timmons was becoming distraught, sadness and grief pushing the tears running down his cheeks. He apologized very softly and sat down.

The entire room was silent. Then Sanouk began to speak. "My mother is fierce in all things. She knew that she would be reunited with my father someday. She told me all about him, and when I saw him for the first time, I knew who he was right away. He was new to being a father, but I was not new to having a father, and that's because of my mother."

Christy watched as several wiped tears from their eyes, even some of the men.

"So last cruise, I was here to give him the sendoff. And just like his life, things happened. But she made me promise that I would tell his story and their love story to all of you. And perhaps to tell it to Gunny one more time." He pointed to the urn that was sitting in front of Christy on the table.

The entire room was with him. Several sighed, some lightly moaned at the touching display of love Sanouk shared with them all.

"So he would not want you to cry. He would not want you to feel like he missed something. He would want you to celebrate who he was and to celebrate each other. Because that's who my father was. And he still is today. I also want to say I am so grateful to my new father, my stepfather, Master Chief Timmons, who was one of his closest friends. He had done his duty well. He is taking very good care of my mother, Gunny's favorite wife."

After Sanouk finished his speech, people ate their dinner timidly, the discussions were nearly whispers. Even the children were quiet. As the tables were being cleared, everyone got together in a group, gathered by the elevators going up to the twelfth level of the ship, and walked to the bow. In a circle, they congregated around Sanouk and Timmons, who held Gunny's ashes in the urn. Timmons released his hold on the canister, and Sanouk unscrewed the bottom. Before releasing the ashes, he said something in Thai that Christy couldn't understand. Then he turned to the crowd and asked for everyone to give a silent prayer and to say hello. Not goodbye, but hello.

Instantly, several of the women wept. Several mouths were covered, but most people bowed their heads in reverence and silence for the life of a man they all missed.

Sanouk waited just a minute or two, turned to the ocean, and released the plug at the bottom of the canister. They all watched as Gunny's gray ashes and clumps of rosebuds from Christy's potpourri flew, escaping to the ocean forever.

Babies cried, kids started running back and forth on the deck, couples kissed, people held hands, men embraced each other, and women kissed each other's cheeks. It was not only a celebration of what had been but a celebration of what was to be.

Christy would never forget that evening as she stood on the bow of the ship in the warm Mexican breeze with her children, the love of her life, and with the other men who would keep her husband safe, no matter what.

She felt no sadness. Only gratitude.

CHAPTER 10

KYLE CALLED A meeting with several of the members of SEAL Team 3 in their private dining room. He promised Christy that he would keep it brief and not get in late. He wanted to spend a little time with her as well.

The dining room had been cleared, and tables had been set for breakfast the next morning. Kyle promised the waiters that they'd remove the chairs from the tables and cluster in a circle in an area away from the dishes. Everybody sat down, and they began.

"First of all, thank you everyone for coming. I just want to say that it has been my honor to be your platoon leader for all these many years, and to some of you, your families and your friendship have grown over many years. I've known some of you more than a decade now. Others, I've just met and began to form fond relationships with. I have to say that this trip has brought to light so many of the things I enjoy about being part of our brotherhood, and it really hit me tonight—even though Gunny'd already gone on years ago—as we physically passed his ashes back into the ocean.

"I realize it more and more every day that life is very short, but the actions we take make it meaningful. I know there's a lot of people out there who don't understand how we could love what we do so much. I know they don't understand why we might choose to leave our families behind or put ourselves in danger for something perhaps we don't even understand. But men like us are not ordinary men. We have extraordinary desires, dreams, commitments. It's being next to some guy who would literally put his life on the line for you. That's the intense level of brotherhood, kinship, and friendship you don't get in the real world. I sometimes wonder to myself what kind of a person I'd be if I ever got off the teams. And no, that's not what I'm about to talk to you about."

"Kyle, I think I speak for everybody here," Cooper began, "when I say we all feel the same way about you. It's an honor to have you as our team leader. I don't think I've ever met a better role model, a better friend, a better level-headed thinker, and I know a lot of it is the luck of the draw. I could have been placed any-where, but for some reason God stuck me here on this team with all you farts too."

Several laughed.

"Now you're going to make me tear up," said T.J.

Fredo fidgeted and added his take. "I get back to my room tonight, fellas, and Mia is going to say, 'No more team meetings. You come home crying when you're with your boyfriends.' She's going to think that's real fucked up."

Again, there was more laughter.

"So what's the big deal, Kyle? I mean, this was something we all had to do together. I didn't know Gunny as well as most of you, but I sure am glad I got to know a lot more about him tonight. And that reminds me, it's the quality of your life. It's who you hang around. I can't ever imagine why I thought I would do something else. But this was special. And these times won't always be this special. There'll be a lot of ups and downs and sadness too." Danny was visibly shaking with the power of his words.

Kyle stood up and paced several steps to the right and then to the left. "I think there's a possibility we were created to take care of and protect the innocent for a reason. And if you think about the cruise that we took nearly ten years ago now, it was sort of divine providence that that ship was the one chosen by the terrorists. I have to tell you I'm getting that feeling again."

Several groans could be heard. A couple guys

swore. T.J. looked at him and shook his head.

"We have fought for the innocents in all that we've done. We've been given tasks to run missions and to protect teachers, aid workers, diplomats, children, doctors, housewives, priests, and people who sell things at open air markets. It's the little people that we serve, right?" Kyle asked.

Several of the men nodded in full agreement.

Kyle continued, "I was belowdecks with Luke today, and after we met with Dr. Bonelli, on our way out, I found—well, we walked past a room that had a door open. Inside, we saw two young women tied up to a bed. They were gagged. One of them had been beaten around the eyes, and she was crying."

Kyle looked down at his feet and waited for the group to settle down a bit. There was quite a bit of whispered anger, swearing, and disbelief.

"I can't just walk away from this. T.J. and I talked to the doctor today, and I don't know what they're going to do, but I promised the doctor that if he didn't report it to the officers on board the ship, I would. And that puts me in a little bit of a difficult situation. I don't really know what's happening there, but I can't just walk away if I think that there's some kind of trafficking going on."

"You got that right," barked Tucker. "None of us could walk away from that. That really pisses me off."

Several others chimed in as well.

Kyle continued, "And all of you know, we were in places in Africa where this was going on, and we've seen firsthand the damage that it does to communities, to families, and especially the women and children that are trafficked."

"Do you think the doctor might be in on it, Kyle?" Cooper asked. "You think it's something that the officers here know about?"

"I don't know. God, I'm hoping not. But I just don't know. I'm going to ask for your support. I don't want to ruin our vacation, but I have to find out about this, and if any of you don't want to be a part of this, you just tell me right now. I'll stop. But just imagine, gents, if that was your wife or one of your daughters. Wouldn't you want somebody to speak up for her?"

"Abso-fucking-lutely we would," agreed Trace.

"That just not acceptable," said Danny.

"So I could do this with a couple of you, but I'd rather tell you all upfront that I want to research and investigate. If we find something going on here, we're going to have to report it, and it's likely the State Department or somebody is going to want us to do something about it. And maybe they won't. But I don't want to enter into this or do research without telling you all what I'm doing. Because whatever any of us does is going to involve us all. We are one family here."

Jamison Daniels leaned forward. "One of the things I noticed about you guys, when I decided to explore trying out for the teams, is this. We are a force for good. Another thing I noticed is that you don't just jump into things half-cocked. You train, you plan, you play hard, you fight hard, and you live life hard. That's what it's all about for me. I don't want an unchaotic life. I've had that. I've had an easy life, and I want a life that means something. I want to be able to do good things for the world. That's why I signed up. And I signed up so I could do it with a bunch of brothers like you guys."

Several 'me too's and 'right on, man's went around the room. The group was solidly behind finding out the truth about the two women, including whether it was widespread or isolated and what the officers on board were going to do about it.

"So, Kyle, I'm onboard this with you," said Tucker. "Brandy, the kids, all the other wives probably feel the same. None of them would want us to just look the other way. And, God, I hope it's not trafficking. I really do. It's something probably sick and twisted, but I hope not a big operation. But somebody who abuses women? He's pretty much garbage in my book."

Tyler, Luke, and Danny, who sat nearby, all laughed. Jason gave him a slap on the back.

Kyle continued. "So we are supposed to leave the

ship at nine o'clock for the day excursions tomorrow morning. I don't know if you guys have signed up for anything, but Christy and I decided we'd take the kids and walk through the artist village on the bus trip and do some shopping. I'm going to find some time to locate Dr. Bonelli first to see if he has anything for me. But then I'm going to go to the officers upstairs, straight to the brass.

"We signed up too," said Trace. "The girls are stoked about doing some shopping."

"I'm going to wait to call the Headshed. Maybe I'll give Collins a call in the morning before we leave the ship, but I'm going to wait to ask for instructions until I know more. What I want all of you guys to do is to also observe. Keep your attentions focused, but don't be obvious. If six or seven of you find yourselves wandering downstairs near the medical office on Deck 2 and you happen to come across room number 2108, which is the room I saw the girls in, maybe we collectively start getting information. I think it's not a good idea to do it tonight. We ought to let things cool off and assume that nothing's going to happen any further. But tomorrow, I want everybody's eyes and ears open, and I want some surveillance done."

"Can I make a suggestion?" Trace asked.

"Sure. What do you have?"

"You know the ladies are really good at digging information up on us."

The group laughed at that one.

Trace continued. "They are so damned intuitive when it comes to things like this that I think we could task them with a little bit of exploration as well. However, we don't get the kids involved. Agreed?"

"Hell yeah," said T.J.

Danny agreed along with Jake and Jamison. "Me too. Count me in," said Tyler.

"This is right up Mia's alley," said Fredo. "She loves to investigate, and if she gets wind that some woman needs help, she's going to be all over that."

Kyle smiled at the group. "Yeah. I thought all of you would feel this way. Let's see what we got, but if there is something going on, I don't think there's a snowball's chance in hell they're going to get away with it."

The meeting adjourned. Kyle approached Cooper to ask about getting some help with a new bandage and tape for Luke.

"No problem, Kyle. Let me grab my bag, and I'll meet you over at your state room in just a few minutes. That okay with you?"

"Yeah, I think Christy and I both would appreciate that. And just check out the puffiness and those stitches. They look really good to me, but I just want to make sure."

"Did you check with her about the shots?"

"I did. He's good."

Kyle walked by himself through the promenade and past the casino, which was going strong now that the ship was sufficiently off the coast of Mexico. Not shopping, gambling, or watching sports games appealed to him. The whole party scene and drinking didn't, either. He'd been sobered by the events of this morning and this afternoon. He wanted to get back with his family. He wanted Luke checked again, and then he wanted to have a talk with Christy. He needed to make sure that she fully understood what he'd seen and what they were going to do as a group.

The kids were tucked into their bunk beds, each boy in separate beds. Maggie took a spot next to Luke on the bottom, but Kyle knew that, after everyone fell asleep, she'd make her way into the bed he shared with Christy. She wasn't going to want to spend all night with their brother.

Cooper knocked on the door, said hello to the family, and sat down ready to take a look at Luke's patch. He removed the gauze and the tape then reapplied a new patch with some smaller pieces of tape that would hold it in place during the night.

"How does it feel, son?" he asked Luke.

"It hurts a little. It feels a little warm. I bumped it a couple of times, but it's okay."

"You feel a little warm, that's true. But I think it's your body's way of fighting infection, Luke. We'll check you in the morning. And hey, you did a great job today keeping it clean."

"Thanks, Mr. Cooper," Luke said.

Cooper messed up his hair and gave him a smile. Standing up, his tall six-foot-four frame was just as skinny as Kyle remembered him the first time he saw Coop in BUD/S training. Ten years had passed since they'd first met each other. Cooper, who didn't drink, hadn't gained more than a pound or two. Kyle had always envied the tall SEAL medic and his calm demeanor.

"Thanks, man," Kyle said.

"No problem," said Coop. "Night, Christy." He respectfully turned his back to give her privacy, and then he left.

Christy had been reading a book, so when Coop left, she set her book down, turned the light out, and asked Kyle if he was going to come to bed.

"Let's step out on the balcony. I want to talk to you in private for a minute," Kyle answered.

A full moon reflected on a very calm Pacific Ocean. Warm pleasant breezes blew from the land. He sat down next to her on the balcony and took her hand.

"Am I going to like this discussion, Kyle?" Her eyes sparkled in the light of the moon. He could smell her faint perfume scent.

"Nothing you can't handle, Mrs. Lansdown. I don't think there's anything you can't handle, Christy. That's one of the things I love about you."

"Are you sure you're not buttering me up for something?" She looked at Kyle sideways and then turned her head the other direction and glanced at him again as if getting another view. "What in the devil are you cooking up here?"

"It's kind of serious, Christy." He looked at their entwined fingers and then spoke softly. "When Luke and I were downstairs, we saw a couple of ladies that were looking like they were in distress. They'd been gagged and bound and were tied to a bed frame. Even Luke saw it."

Christy put her palm to her mouth. "Good Lord, so that's what he was talking about. He said that you met a very bad man, and I was hoping it wasn't the doctor."

"No, that's a whole other issue, but these two girls were underage. I'm sure of it. And if they are kidnapped victims, I think it's incumbent on us to research what's going on here. As you know, several of our other missions involved human trafficking, and if the ship is somehow involved in that, that's something our government should know about. It violates ethics and morals, not to mention criminal statutes. We're in international waters now, and the ship is an Italian registry, but it caters to American citizens who are on board. And that becomes of interest to our government."

"Do you think that's going on?" she asked.

"No, I don't. I think it could be just two girls, maybe just a case of them being in the wrong place and stupid about their choices. I don't know, but I have to check it out in case it's more. And let's face it, when is it too little or too many? Is it right for even one woman to have to put up with that kind of treatment?"

"Well, you know exactly how I feel, Kyle. I say go for it. And I'm going to back you up one hundred percent."

"Yes, I knew that." He brushed her cheek. "But I wanted to hear you say it, sweetheart. And we're going to try to do it in such a way that it doesn't affect the kids or the vacation. But you know me. I saw an injustice happening, and I can't walk away from it. That's just who I am."

"And that's why I love you. Count me in, Kyle. What do you want me to tell the wives?"

"Everybody's talking tonight. We want you to keep your eyes and ears open. Without the kids, we'd like you to investigate when we are on board, and then tomorrow night, we'll decide what course of action to take. But one way or the other, we're going to make sure the captain and all the junior officers on the ship know what we've discovered. And until they do a thorough investigation, we're not going to give up."

Christy smiled, musing to herself, and searched the silver sea in front of her. She tilted her head back to look at the moon, whispering, "Well then, I'm glad we sent Gunny off today. He didn't need to know about all this. And he doesn't need to be involved in it. I'm glad that nothing interfered with that service today. Thank you, Kyle."

CHAPTER 11

B REAKFAST TIME WAS always an interesting time for
Christy and her brood. Used to getting to the
office first thing when Kyle was home, she often
directed traffic but didn't stay to watch Kyle overrule
her. He was known for taking their healthy meals and
turning them into lavish pancake and bacon feasts that
the kids loved. The oatmeal was often tossed, and
scrambled eggs were squarely at the bottom of the food
popularity list.

Today, they were heading out for some shopping
and exploration in the little artist village near Cabo San
Lucas, Todos Santos. It was to be an hour-plus bus ride
from the pier with time left over to wander the streets
in Cabo before getting back on the ship. So Christy
diligently made sure the kids had enough to eat for a
great morning start.

Brandon and Ali had continued their active friendship and, while not pre-teen age yet, had begun to

develop an interest in some of the older young teen girls on the cruise, so they began spying on them. Being rebuffed at just about every turn didn't quell their ardor, and if they weren't invited to the party, they could make a splash, drenching sunbathers nearby, which was their most favorite way of getting even.

But it wasn't the only way.

Ali was trying to show Brandon how to use his slingshot, the toy Danny had made for him years ago in Iraq. Both boys had younger brothers, and often the projectiles they were trying to launch were soft, their targets being the younger brothers Luke and Griffin. Griffin was used to Ali's constant teasing, but Luke didn't take to the punishment as well. He came running to Christy when he'd been hit in the forehead with a pat of butter on their first breakfast outing.

Today, the older boys were going to launch an all-out attack on the "mean girls," as they called them—all girls from other families and not from the Community. They made bombs of jam and butter, added cold cereal fruit rings for weight, and sometimes rolled these little balls in sugar for the effect they made when landing. It was as close to an explosion as they could get with the materials they had to work with.

In order to achieve the success they were looking for, the boys had to reposition themselves several times after launch, so they would avoid detection.

Christy was vaguely aware of what was going on. Luci Begay, Ali's mother, was also watching with some apprehension, waiting for everything to escalate.

Danny and Kyle and several others were having custom omelets created for them and were standing in line, oblivious to the impending danger.

"I wish Kyle would get back over here. You seeing what I'm seeing?" Christy asked Luci.

"I'm on it. They've been rather busy creating these flying rockets. We're going to have to stop it pretty soon now. But I'm curious, aren't you?" Luci answered her, her eyes sparkling. "I guess deep down inside, I don't want to spoil their fun. As long as no one gets hurt."

"Yeah, but soon. all of the kids will want one, and Danny's going to be very busy making them weapons. And of course, the staff are not going to tolerate it. I pray it doesn't go too far over the edge."

But Christy had that impending doom feeling in the pit of her stomach that all would go to hell very soon.

She didn't have to wait long.

The first projectile hit one of the pre-teen girls in the back between her shoulder blades. The smear of strawberry jam and marshmallow sauce fanned out and actually looked like a real wound from a distance.

But it was her scream that got everyone's attention. The girl jumped to her feet and hopped around as if she'd actually been hurt. Everyone in the area was focused on her. When Christy looked for the boys, they were nowhere to be found.

She saw Luke sitting all alone, having been abandoned, and motioned for him to come over. Maggie left her circle of friends and joined him at her side. Christy leaned into Luci. "Where are they now? Did you see them run off?"

"I missed it." She stood and scanned the room, shaking her head.

The parade of men, carrying their heaping plates of food, soon arrived. Kyle had just sat down when Christy had to break the news to him.

"…and I can't find him anywhere."

"Oh, let them be for a little bit. They're not harming anyone. Just being boys."

"Kyle, you know this isn't going to end well."

He sighed, stopped to look at his almost untouched omelet, and answered, "I'd like just a few more bites of this delicious creation, and then I'll go find him." He gave her the smile she could never resist. "I'll take over from here. No worries."

Luci and Christy shared a look. Danny was seated with Griffin, helping him finish his breakfast.

Another wad of something sticky and bright red

landed on the middle of the girls' table, and this time, all five of them stood up, objected loudly, scanned the room, and began to point. Christy followed the trajectory and saw the swinging door to the wait staff area move, followed by the sound of a crash of dishes.

"That's it. They've done it now," Christy mumbled, furious.

Kyle grabbed her arm, holding her from springing on the boys. "Let me do it. Only one way they're getting out of there, and I'm sure they'll be escorted back in about thirty seconds after they get a good scolding."

Christy studied the doorway as Luke asked her, "Mom, is Brandon in trouble?"

"Yes. He. Is."

"Will he get a spanking?" He appeared eager to view such corporal punishment.

"I'd say the odds are good, buddy," Kyle interjected. "Let's give it another minute or two. Finish your breakfast."

But still the boys did not surface.

"Do you think they're okay in there?" Christy asked her husband.

"There they are," said Luci, pointing to the second-story dining area.

"How the hell did they get up there?" Kyle asked.

Luke had the answer. "There's this ladder thingy

they use to bring stuff upstairs, so they don't have to walk up the steps. Brandon showed it to me yesterday. I was too scared to jump on it."

"They rode the dumbwaiter?" Christy asked.

"What's a dumbwaiter?" asked Luke.

"Something you'll never have to worry about." Kyle stood up, readying himself to bring the boys back just before they launched another projectile on two of the girls leaving the dining room.

Ali's calculation wasn't as accurate as it should be, and instead of hitting the girls, it landed squarely at the throat of a short waiter balancing a large tray with dirty dishes on it. The waiter went down with another huge crash.

"Kyle!"

"I'm on it." He was halfway across the room already and then bent down on one knee to help the waiter stand back up. He was animated but unharmed. Two other wait staff were quickly picking up broken dishes, and the dining room manager was plowing through the gawking crowd like a torpedo.

Christy looked up in the balcony and saw both the boys slink down the stairwell, hanging onto the brass railing. They quietly returned to her side.

"Honestly, Ali, you know better than this," started Luci. "You're staying on board. No road trip for you!"

"Mom, I missed. I didn't do it on purpose."

"That's my point, Ali. You never should have been doing it in the first place."

"Brandon," Christy began, "you guys were riding the dumbwaiter?"

"We do it all the time, Mom. It's fun."

"It's dangerous. You're not allowed on that thing. What do you two think you are, a couple of monkeys? You're acting like spoiled brats. This isn't how we've raised you."

Kyle managed to apologize to the room manager, who had been waving his arms and pointing to the kitchen door.

In the end, they shook hands. Kyle apologized again to the waiter, who bowed and seemed to be very uncomfortable being in the limelight before he quickly disappeared.

At the table, Kyle yanked Brandon up by the collar and left the room, followed by Danny and Ali.

The ensuing laughter from some of the other parents, as if this was some orchestrated floor show, didn't help Christy's mood. She second-guessed her decision to bring the kids, with Luke's injury and now this.

"I can tell this is going to be a very long day," she mumbled to her oatmeal.

THE LOGISTICS OF having Brandon left behind on the ship, since the Children's Center was closed for the day, was too difficult to work out. Christy didn't want anyone else in the group to be responsible for him, so it was decided that Brandon would come with them today on shore.

Nearly two-thirds of their group boarded the two buses for the Todos Santos village tour. Kyle and Christy sat behind Brandon and Luke. Maggie sat on her mom's lap and promptly fell asleep.

"Has anyone been able to get in touch with the doctor?"

"Nope. He hasn't returned my call, either. I'm guessing I'll be meeting with the captain tonight. Perfect timing, too, because it's the captain's dinner."

"I imagine he'll be thrilled," she said, rolling her eyes at her husband.

"We'll see. They had time to off-load the girls at the dock early this morning or even yesterday at the pickup. They could be long gone, so it's going to be hard to prove, but we'll launch an inquiry anyway."

"You did what you could."

"I have this feeling in my gut that I don't like. But part of me definitely hopes there's nothing to see."

"That would make sense," Christy mused. "Afterall, we are supposed to be on vacation. A cruise is not supposed to be a high contact sport. There aren't devils under every rock. Maybe this is a good wakeup call for you to just relax and enjoy yourself."

"But I can't until I know."

"But, Kyle, you're going to ruin it for everyone else, too, if you're not careful."

"They don't feel that way. How come you do?" His look was angry. Instead of cooling the flame, she'd enraged him again.

Christy knew it was a control issue. He liked information, craved it even. He wasn't going to back down until he'd been convinced what he saw was rotten consensual behavior. Because the girls looked underage, he couldn't let it go.

"I know you only want what's right. I respect that. But if you don't get straight answers, it doesn't have to mean there's a conspiracy going on. Not every ship carries trafficked humans, Kyle. You know this."

He put his arm around her. "Maybe you're right. We've seen so much, though. It's a losing war, and I never thought I'd be saying this. Modern day slavery. It was wrong then, and it's wrong now."

"And I know Brandon isn't helping things, either." Brandon looked over his shoulder as he heard his name.

Kyle leaned forward. "You going to behave?" His words were pointed, but his face was soft, filled with love for their son, no matter what.

"Yessir. Besides, you confiscated Ali's sling shot."

"His dad has it," corrected Kyle. "And that's where

it's going to stay the whole rest of the trip."

"Do you suppose you could make me one when we get back to San Diego? I think I would be good at it."

"We'll see. All depends on your behavior, Brandon."

After the youngster turned around, Christy kissed Kyle on the cheek.

"Thanks for doing this, Christy. For arranging this beautiful vacation. I think we need to do more," he sighed.

"You're right. I think if we did more of this, the family vacation travel will stop looking like another mission. And now you're looking for the fight, aren't you?"

"No, I just want to be sure that innocent girls aren't being abused."

She laid her head against his shoulder, repositioned Maggie on her lap, and hoped that all the drama of the trip was behind them.

CHAPTER 12

THE TRIP TO Todos Santos was uneventful, which allowed Kyle to actually relax for the first time since boarding the ship. Christy and the kids had a good time wandering through stalls in the large open-air market and picking up pieces of pottery, jewelry, and little handmade toys, sometimes sold to Kyle's children by children of the same age from Mexico. It was a rich, cultural eye candy type of place and not at all like some of the places Kyle had visited in Africa, Cape Verde, or the Canary Islands.

Several of the other team members who took the same bus trip frequented the same shops, and it was like their outings in San Diego. The kids played in the park together, and the women sat outside enjoying the sun and the delightful environs. Kyle knew that this wasn't the real world. It was an illusion. But for a day, he could forget all that. He could pretend there weren't evildoers in the world, intent on making money at the expense of others.

Because the wives and children were present, the SEALs watched their language, didn't drink as much, and spent most of their time focusing on their own families. But there was a natural pull, and on several occasions, they would offer to take care of several of the kids so that a few of the men could explore some other part of the marketplace together.

Laden with bags of colorful clothing and trinkets, Kyle and Christy and their brood took the first bus back to the outskirts of Cabo. There had been a jitney set up that would take them directly to the ship, and Christy offered to take the bags, leaving Kyle and the kids behind. But he overruled that plan, took the bags himself, and promised to meet her back at a restaurant.

As he rode the little cart headed for the gangway, Kyle examined the cargo hold that was open, exchanging goods and supplies as it always was when they hit land. Nothing caught his eye as far as unusual activity, and he was looking for it, too. He didn't see any underage women going in or out of the hold, and he didn't notice any kind of contraband being loaded up or anything looking suspicious. But he also knew that there was no way in the world he would ever be able to tell, since everything was wrapped in plastic, loaded onto storage containers, or boxed on pallets that were then lifted aboard ship.

At the gangway, he brought his bags in, put them through the X-ray machine, showed his badge, and was given entrance. Back in his room, he stowed the packages and decided to take a quick trip downstairs just to examine the area where the room and medical offices were. In the hallway, he found Coop.

"Hey, I thought you guys were downtown," he said to Coop's back.

Coop turned around and clasped hands with Kyle. "Well, I guess I could ask the same thing about you, but Libby and the kids are waiting for me. I just came back to bring the packages."

"Oh, so the Lansdownes and the Coopers might be having a shopping pissing contest, that what you're saying?" Kyle asked.

"You could say that." Coop grinned. "Unfortunately, I think Libby's got you beat."

Several minutes later, as they waited by the elevators, Kyle approached the subject of the girls. "You know, I was going to take a quick gander downstairs. You want to come?"

Coop rolled his shoulders, "I think I probably better escort you. God knows what kind of trouble you could get into, Lansdowne."

"That's for sure." Kyle punched the button for Deck 2, and they waited for the elevator doors to open.

Downstairs, the scene was much less crowded than

before. The place almost looked abandoned. There were no long lines of pallet operators or sounds of forklifts moving heavy boxes from one storage area to another. The entryway was guarded by two ships officers, and the pallets that had been brought aboard were still waiting for someone to take them to the storage hold. They were wrapped tightly in heavy plastic. It appeared most of the crew had been granted leave, or at least time off on shore.

From previous trips Kyle had taken, he was aware of the fact that most of the crew, if they were going to wire money home or make telephone calls, had to use a designated shipper's office in town, sponsored by the cruise line, and many of the crew would be attending to business that way.

Kyle showed Cooper the hallway, glanced at door number 2108, and then continued down until they came to the medical office door. The door was shut with a sign indicating office hours would resume later on in the evening.

He knocked on the door anyway and waited. When no one answered, he turned and directed Cooper back down the hallway toward the stateroom he had been at before.

"You think I should knock?" Kyle asked.

"Your funeral," said Coop. He looked down the hallway in both directions. "I don't see anybody checking on things. Nobody seems to care, so yeah, I'd go ahead."

Kyle rapped on the door briskly. There were sound of someone flushing a toilet and then running the water on the other side of the door. A few seconds later, someone muttered something through the door in a male voice, the language one Kyle didn't understand.

When the door opened a crack, Kyle could see it was not the same individual he had seen the day before. "Excuse me, is this your room?" he asked.

"Yes. Yes." He didn't look anything like the beefy fellow from yesterday. He was a very slight Korean or Chinese worker who wore a white cook staff uniform jacket. He opened the doorway slightly, and Kyle peered inside but did not see any evidence of anyone else there. It did appear that all four beds had been used, however.

"How long? How many days?" Kyle asked.

"We go thirty-seven days," he said in choppy English. "Then no ship, and then we go six months more."

"No, I meant how long have you been here?"

At first, the man didn't appear to understand what Kyle was asking him. Coop attempted to clarify, and then the man's face lit up.

"Ah! I come here today." He pointed to the floor. "We all come—there are five of us; we take turns—we came today, together from another ship."

Obviously, they'd rearranged the room, or perhaps the girls with the occupant had been offloaded. Kyle realized they were going to have even more difficulty investigating what he thought he had seen now.

"Thank you. I was looking for the man who was here before. Do you know him?"

"No." The man shook his head then gave a slight bow. "So sorry. I not know anybody on this ship, except my friends. Cousins."

"Thank you. So sorry to bother you, then," Kyle said as he closed the door. He pointed down towards the elevators.

"So I gather that's not the guy." Coop walked briskly alongside him.

"Nope. Back to square one, I guess."

They approached the elevator lobby, went up one deck, and exited through the main gangway on Deck 3, waving to several who had returned from town for the day. As they walked down toward the pier, Kyle said, "I think Christy was probably right about this."

"About what?"

The two of them sat in the back seat of the little truck jitney, which drove them toward the gate.

"Well, she told me I was making up conspiracies and that I needed to relax a little bit. I think maybe she has a point there, don't you?"

"Well, you had to check it out. That's what you said you'd do; I don't think there was any harm in that. And if I know you, Kyle, you're still going to report it."

"You got that right."

They hopped off the jitney and strolled several blocks until Kyle found the park with the restaurant overlooking where he had agreed to meet Christy and the kids. Several other families were also there, having snacks and some canned drinks. Coop said farewell, in search of Libby and his two kids.

Christy handed him her Coke, adding, "I was thinking we could go to a museum. They have a cultural museum featuring children artists, and it's just a block away. I thought it would be good for the kids. What do you think, Kyle?"

"Sure, I'm up for anything, but we don't have much time—maybe an hour or so." He watched as locals and several other tourists from the ship passed by slowly. He was aware of Christy's eyes on him.

"What?" he asked.

"Just checking." Christy kissed him on the cheek again. "I wanted to make sure that was a real smile. A real vacation smile this time."

"Are we having fun yet?" he asked.

"Yes, my love, we are. And you're doing great."

AT DINNER, KYLE attempted to speak with several of the

senior officers. Although the captain was supposed to attend his own dinner, he was not present. The unfriendly chief engineer greeted him frostily. The whole group was herded quickly through the receiving line and then were handed champagne for a "Captain's Traditional Toast" without the captain. It wasn't lost on the rest of the team when the doors were closed. They'd been essentially separated from the rest of the cruise guests. Kyle knew this wasn't normal.

They felt it had been billed incorrectly, since there was no dinner prepared. One of the junior officers held up his glass and spoke to them all.

"We welcome you, this unique group, to our little ship and hope that you are having a restful and relaxing time. I hope you will excuse our Italian informal style, but due to the large nature of your group, your special Captain's Dinner is being prepared in your own private dining room, since it can accommodate you all together."

As he expected, all the men were on their best behavior, and no one grumbled.

Still holding his glass high, he raised it higher still. "So we salute you, members of SEAL Team 3. The honor is all ours for the gift of your presence. Salut."

"Salut," the group repeated as everyone drank together.

"Unfortunately, Captain Antonini has been called

away on an emergency and will be unable to attend your dinner this evening, but he promises to make it a point to meet you all in person during the remainder of the cruise."

Kyle glanced between the men, carefully masking any feelings he didn't want to show. He was certain all the men felt the same way he did. This "emergency" might have something to do with what Kyle planned to speak to the captain about this evening. It was no coincidence. Even Christy gave him a strange glance, raising one eyebrow.

They finished their champagne, and one-by-one, each of the officers left the small dining area. No additional glasses or hors d'oeuvres were offered to the SEALs. Their empty glasses were collected, and then they were ushered outside the door by white-tuxed waiters wearing white gloves.

"You will please proceed to your dining room for the special meal prepared for you now," said one of the waiters.

"Do you get the impression they didn't intend on having much of a conversation with us?" T.J. whispered in his ear.

"Let's just play along with it. But I'd like to know who found out about us."

"You kind of spilled the beans, Kyle, from what T.J. says, when you talked to the doctor," said Coop.

"I hate it when that happens," mumbled Kyle.

Christy turned around and glared at all three of them. She put her fingers to her lips.

"By the way, where is the doc?" T.J. asked, again incurring a frown from Christy.

"Getting ready for his office hours?" Coop guessed. This time, he was extra quiet.

The display awaiting them in their private room was every bit as spectacular as had been expected. In the center of each table was a large silver-footed platter holding an overflow of lobster—at least more than one per person seated at each of the tables. They were serenaded by a pair of dueling violinists, who wafted around the chairs and picked out ladies to make love to with their instruments. Kyle was amused at some of the expressions on his teammates' faces as the ladies soaked it up and his buds nearly grabbed the bows and wrapped it around the slick-down violinists' throats.

Dessert was served on silver platters decorated with sparklers. Bottles of Italian wines were served in unlimited capacities, including the dessert muscats. At the very end, they were served cigars and expressly told only to smoke them outside.

Kyle noted Sanouk had ingested way too much wine. He picked up a handful of cigars and placed them in his pocket. The attendant didn't blink.

Christy looked beautiful as ever, her face and arms

reddened by the exposure to sun during their shopping and walking tour. Kyle had never seen her so happy.

"Taking a dose of your own advice, I see," he whispered to her ear.

"I am. I think the wine is helping a bit, though."

She faced him, the familiar spark between them igniting his libido.

"You're looking especially ravishing tonight, Mrs. Lansdowne," he whispered back, kissing her gently on the lips.

"Really? I was thinking about taking a little stroll to lifeboat number twenty-six tonight. Care to join me?"

"I thought you'd never ask." He started to help her up when he received a note in a sealed envelope with a scripted "A" on the front. He opened it and discovered a private, written invitation to go upstairs to the bridge, signed by Captain Antonini.

"What is it?" she asked.

"I'm afraid I have something I have to do first. Can I meet you up there later? Shall I text you for our little liaison?"

"Where are you going?" she asked again.

He handed her the note.

"The captain?"

Kyle shrugged. "It shouldn't be too long. But don't wait up, just in case."

"Don't go alone, Kyle." He could see the concern in

her eyes.

"Not to worry." He stood, gave her a kiss, and then went over to speak to T.J. and Coop, who also got up and followed him out into the main dining room to the promenade level.

Captain Antonini was an extremely handsome, older man dressed in a deep navy-blue uniform, complete with intricate gold braiding and brass buttons. He sat in the corner in a rounded-back red club chair, his legs crossed, waiting for them. Calmly, he sipped an espresso. His second was steering the ship, taking the vessel on to Puerto Vallarta for tomorrow's planned shore excursions.

Kyle knew it was the custom the captain rarely took the helm, as long as he was present for important decisions. Two other officers were seated nearby, monitoring various screens, including a series of navigation maps which displayed their position in relation to several other vessels in the area, small islands, hazards, and other land masses. Another sat behind a console wearing headphones.

"Sir, we have three gentlemen here to see you, at your request." The young junior officer announced them and then left.

Captain Antonini stood, shaking their hands. He handed his coffee cup to an attendant and then invited them outside to the bridge deck and past a uniformed guard, who stepped aside and allowed the four of them entry through the doorway of his private quarters. He had a small, black marble dining table, which seated four, with brightly colored upholstered chairs position at each side. He closed the door behind them and locked it.

The men remained standing.

"I am speaking to you this evening out of a sense of loyalty and duty, because I understand that you, Mr. Lansdowne, have had a very illustrious career in the military, and I respect that."

"Thank you, sir. I also respect your position here. Might I ask, do you have military background as well?"

"I do. I am an Italian by birth, but I have been an officer on several Naval and private vessels, none of them Italian, unfortunately. I have been deployed for maneuvers all over the world, cruising under different flags. This is my semi-retirement, and it is also one of my last voyages."

Kyle could see the reason for the secrecy. "May I then introduce you to two other men on SEAL Team 3? This is T.J. Talbot and Calvin Cooper. Both of these men have served with me for nearly ten years and are Navy medics."

Captain Antonini shook their hands again and acknowledged them very soberly. "Please, gentlemen, I'd like to keep this rather informal, if you don't mind.

Won't you have a seat, and would you like a drink of some kind?" He motioned to the overstuffed club chairs.

Cooper and T.J. accepted a beer, Kyle asked for a glass of water, but Captain Antonini poured himself a scotch. He sat down on a tall red leather reading chair, sipping his drink.

Kyle studied his personal space, which was appointed with plaques, statues, medals, trophies, and pictures of himself standing beside elites of society, heads of state, and beautiful women.

"I see you have noticed my rogues' gallery here," he gestured toward his decorated walls, waving his hand in the air across his photos and keepsakes from afar. He smiled. "I have lived a very full and rich life. I have been present at the dawns of many histories, and I have enjoyed my travels around the world. I've gotten to meet incredible people, as well as some very evil and small-minded but powerful men."

He leaned back in the chair, crossed his legs, set his drink on the reading table beside him, and examined his nails before he began. "It is funny. When you anticipate the end of your life, you think that its value is the sum total of all of the significant events that occurred while you were living it, but, as it turns out, that doesn't begin to make up for the feeling that, as you grow older, you lose your power. You become comfortable with just fading away."

"You are ill, sir? I'm sorry for that."

"Yes, I'll explain in a minute, but first, I need to bring up another topic."

Kyle wasn't sure where he was going with this. But he respected the man's presence and decided to stay silent.

"I have been told by my chief of engineering that you had some concerns about a particular person, a crew member on this ship, and whether or not he has brought unsuitable women with him."

"I did not mention that to him, sir," Kyle answered. "I merely stated that I had questions for the doctor. I wasn't—"

"Yes, I believe he told me that too," Antonini interrupted and then allowed Kyle to explain.

"I was concerned the women were being abused. And they looked very young and in distress. In fact, they were gagged. One was crying, and she looked to have been struck across her cheek."

"That is a most disturbing accusation, Mr. Lansdowne."

"I agree. I'm glad you feel the same way. I—"

"My chief engineer did not believe this to be true. He didn't believe you."

"But as I said, we didn't discuss this with him." Kyle stopped and reframed the question. "Sir, if I may ask, what is the purpose of this get-together?"

"I have thrown Mr. Scalzi off the ship."

"Mr. Scalzi?"

"The crew member. As you saw this evening, I have kept my chief engineer for now."

Kyle was startled with his statement. "Well, that's—"

"And I have been told we returned the two girls that he may have brought on board to the authorities in Mexico, at Cabo. I have been assured that they will be returned to their families, and I am here to let you know that I did not know that this was occurring. But when Dr. Bonelli brought it to my attention that you had noticed it—"

"Yes. We spoke to him. T.J. and I spoke to him."

"They researched this information before they brought it to me, and it was my decision to have him thrown off the ship. I am fairly certain that he will face some sort of judgment in Mexico, but I wanted you to understand, and I wanted to keep this extremely private. I don't tolerate this sort of behavior. And I want to also reassure you, as I have been assured, that there are no other incidences of women being abused on this ship. I understand from Dr. Bonelli that you alluded to that in some fashion. I am told there is no longer any need to worry further."

"Well, I thank you, sir, and this is quite a surprise, as you can see. Since, as you say, the situation has been handled, then I have no further complaint."

"But I have one more request of you, and when I

found out that I had some fifty-three SEALs and their families on board my ship, I have to tell you that it got my attention. I'm not willing to divulge this to anybody outside this room, but I need to reveal something very private, to be held in very strict confidence. Do I have your word?"

"Of course," Kyle answered. Coop and T.J. did as well.

"I know that my company's cruise lines are being used to traffic humans. They bring them from the United States to Mexico, and they bring them from Mexico to the United States. They travel to South America, and others of this cruise line travel back and forth from Italy and Africa to South America and the Caribbean. I am aware of this because of my senior position, but there has never been a suspicion that the Romancia Italiana has ever been involved in such trafficking."

Kyle stared back at the captain. "Well, yeah, especially since this is a brand new ship."

Captain Antonini sighed. "I should say any ship I've commanded, excuse me. I'm also aware there have been several undercover operations shut down by the company hierarchy. Several senior officers have lost their positions. I am not one of them, and I wish to retire with a perfect record."

"Well, Captain Antonini, we're just here for a family vacation. We cannot be employed since we already work for our government and the Navy. We only wanted to bring this abuse to your attention," Kyle explained.

"I understand, and I am only asking you, as a favor, to investigate further and make sure that Dr. Bonelli and my chief engineer are telling me the truth."

"Do you have reason to suspect them of something?"

"I'm not quite sure who to trust at the present time. You see, your little discovery has made me concerned."

"But I have no authority here. And you wouldn't want to give me that authority nor can you," Kyle corrected.

"That is not necessarily true. I am entrusted to provide for the safety of my passengers. That is my primary concern. I am asking for you to go outside 'the lines' to see what I cannot. I walk down the hallways, and I don't see the same things that you do. I know from your experience that you probably have a sixth sense of such things. I'm only asking for you to generate information if you can. I am giving you access to the ship's cargo data." He pulled out a thumb drive.

"This is a record of all the onboarding and offloading we have done to date for the Romancia. I need someone I can trust to examine the entries and the manifest lists. Perhaps your friends in Washington can help with identifying the names of some of our suppliers to determine if they are all legitimate. And then, should we uncover something nefarious, I would like you to take that information and report it to your government."

"Why wouldn't you do that, Captain? Report it to your cruise line?"

"Because, gentlemen, I might be dead by that time. I want to be sure this information gets out to your government after I retire. We return to San Diego in three days. Then we head up to San Francisco after that, and then I'm done. My career is over. I will probably spend the rest of my life in an alternative treatment cancer clinic in Northern California. For, you see, I am terminally ill and have less than sixty days to live. It's all been arranged."

"I'm so sorry, sir," Kyle said. "Why do you wish to do this now? I mean, shouldn't you just be focused on your own health? Isn't there someone at your company who could better handle such an investigation?"

"You mean let someone else worry about it? You want to know my motivation?"

"Please."

"It's true, these end-of-life decisions are inconvenient for me. But you see, there's one thing that I have never been able to fix. Although I have commanded many ships and had a wonderful life, I could not save the one person in my life who meant the most to me. You see, my wife and granddaughter were kidnapped while on vacation when I was out to sea. My wife was killed, and my granddaughter kidnapped and sold into slavery. I have been told that she perished somewhere in North America, but I have no proof."

"I'm so sorry. When did this happen?"

"It was approximately five years ago. I have exhausted a small fortune trying to uncover the persons who did this with no luck. And now I have no time. However, in the process, I recently learned this cruise line was possibly complicit. I held my tongue until I had the means to be able to get even. I planned to write a report before my death and send it to Washington. But now that you are here, I would like to see you and your team deliver that message for me. Help me make them pay. I want it done legally. I want them shut down and exposed, so that no other women ever receive the kind of treatment that my wife and granddaughter did."

He handed the thumb drive to Kyle, who reluctantly took it. "I'm going to have to check with my superiors, Captain Antonini. I'm not sure what they will say."

"But will you try? Will you try to help me? Would you refuse the wish of a dying man seeking to avenge the deaths of his innocent loved ones?"

CHAPTER 13

CHRISTY HAD FALLEN asleep with a book on her lap, her head at an uncomfortable angle wedged between the headboard mirror and the wall sconce. She awoke and scanned the room, finding all three children fast asleep, oblivious to the reading light.

She switched it off and shuffled to the cabin door, passing the empty bathroom, and peered down the hallway to the right and around the corner to the short hallway on her left. There was no sign of Kyle.

Some vacation this is turning out to be. She'd been telling herself it was impossible lightning would strike twice in the same place, but it did appear as though Kyle had gotten involved in another mission—*on their vacation!*

Crawling back to bed, she lay gazing at the white ceiling, light reflecting from the ship above and below. The powerful rumble of her engines told her they'd picked up speed, heading for their next port.

Many of the other men had been able to spend more time with their families than Kyle had, and as their LPO, she accepted this as normal. But it didn't make it fair nor did she like it. And the more she thought about it, the angrier she got.

She knew it was wrong to feel cheated. Maybe the fact that she'd worked so hard to plan this cruise combined with her high expectations since they hadn't been on a real vacation in months contributed to her rancor, but her mood was getting worse and worse.

She tore the covers off, opened their tiny refrigerator, and pulled out a bottle of liquor she couldn't see in the dark. She screwed open the top and downed what must have been whiskey—a taste she didn't really like. That made her mad too. She punched the bed and then allowed her tears to tumble down, knowing she was helpless to change anything about what was happening on the trip. Was she saying she wished Kyle could just keep a blind eye to things he saw that he knew was wrong? Of course not! But were his own thoughts playing tricks on him? Was it all his over-active imagination?

But then she thought about Luke, who had been so descriptive of the scene they both witnessed. The "bad man" was scary, he'd said. The lady was crying, he'd said.

She heard a door slam and the sounds of soft voices

speaking next door. If Coop was back, then perhaps Kyle would follow soon.

Just then, their cabin door opened, and Kyle quietly closed it behind him.

"Hey there," she whispered.

"Hi," he said, sitting on the bed, removing his shoes. He turned towards her. "I'm so sorry, Christy. I'll tell you in the morning, okay?"

She whispered back, hoping he couldn't see that her face had turned red from crying, "You're really going to leave it like that? Not tell me a thing? I've been worried, Kyle. Honey, this is no fun for the kids or for me—"

She regretted the words as soon as they left her mouth.

"Shhh, I'm so sorry, Christy. I don't want to wake the kids."

Her eyes erupted. She sniffled, wiping her cheeks with the backs of her hands. "I'm losing it, Kyle. I've been so worried. I'm the one responsible for this trip, and with all the children and the spouses, I just feel horrible that this has turned into another mission, except we're all baggage now, just in your way. This isn't what our family is all about, Kyle. We don't do missions. We nearly lost everything ten years ago on that last cruise. Is it happening all over again? Or were you guys just hanging out, drinking upstairs?"

"Christy, Christy," he said softly, reaching for her, but she scrambled out of bed and stood, staring at the glistening fast-moving water outside the glass doorway to the balcony.

Kyle was at her back in a flash. His warm arms wrapped around her body, his lips kissing her neck. But all it did was make her more miserable. She couldn't stop crying.

"I know it's a lot on you. Would you like me to tell you what's going on? I just thought you'd sleep better if we discussed it in the morning, sweetheart."

She kept her back to him as he rubbed her upper arms and warmed her backside with his hard body pressed against hers. She wanted to melt but felt frozen in place. Finally, after taking several deep breaths, her tears stopped.

"Tell me. I need to know. How bad is it?"

"Come on." He took her hand, reached for the blanket on the bed, opened the slider, and ushered her outside, wrapping the blanket around her shoulders. "Let's sit, okay, honey?"

The chair was wet and cold, but she plunked herself down as he sat beside her, moving his chair close and then re-wrapping them both in the blanket. The air had turned cold, and the moon was partially obscured by large storm clouds. She stuffed down the brief concern that perhaps they'd get some serious rain and rough seas ahead.

Oh dammit, Christy. Lighten up!

"Tell me, Kyle."

"Okay."

He cleared his throat, which made Christy nervous.

"We met with the captain who told us that, because of my report to the doctor, the crew member was tossed off the ship and the two women he brought on board were returned to authorities in Cabo San Lucas. We don't have any details except the captain was led to believe they were victims of this crewmember, and he'll face punishment for it. And yes, they were probably under the age of consent."

"Well, that's a good thing, right?" she whispered back. "That didn't need to take—what?—two hours. He could have just written you that in the letter."

"It's more complicated than that," Kyle answered.

"Of course it is." Her spine was firm, ramrod straight as she clutched the blanket around her body, pulling it up to her neck. Now she was freezing. It was going to be hard to mask her anger. "Just tell me, dammit."

He drew his arm around her shoulder and she didn't respond back to him. He kissed her ear and pressed the side of his head against hers. "I wish— Maybe next time we should go camping. Go somewhere there is no internet, no kids, no team guys, no high seas. Some place safe from all the evil and wrong in the world."

"Where would that be?" She turned to see his face illuminated in the soft lighting of the ship and welcomed the warmth and love she had for him back into her heart. And then it started to seem so funny.

She kissed him. And then she kissed him deeper as his hand found her right breast. Her body began to heat to him, respond, until she remembered he was in the middle of telling her something she wanted to hear.

She pulled away. "Tell me. You've got thirty seconds, or I'm tossing you overboard, sailor."

He chuckled. "I'm impossible, aren't I? I don't deserve you, Christy."

Now she was annoyed. Big. Time. "You better fucking tell me, or you'll be jerking off in the shower for the next month, Kyle Lansdowne."

That made her happy. It also got Kyle's attention.

"Yes, ma'am. Well, the captain asked a special favor of us. He has reason to believe that the company he works for, the cruise line, is somehow involved in human trafficking, and he asked us to look into it for him."

"But—"

"I know, I know. I started telling him the same thing you're thinking, Christy. Here's what's complicated. The man is dying. He says he has sixty days to live. This is his last command, and after that, he'll be attempting some alternative cancer therapy, which he doesn't expect will work, and he'll be gone. He wants us to expose this or get enough information so perhaps the Feds or someone can intervene and catch these guys."

"And you believe that story?"

"I do. Turns out, he's lost his wife and granddaughter to these cretins. He says it happened when he was at sea."

She watched his face in profile now as he searched the clouds and the sea below.

"God, Christy, if something like that happened to you, I'd spend my last days hunting and punishing those who did it. I understand how he feels. And he's almost out of time."

She laid her head against his shoulder. If she'd heard the story from anyone else, she wouldn't have believed it. But Kyle was one of the best people she knew at reading people and assessing their truthfulness. If he believed it, then Christy knew there wasn't anything in the world that would stop him. It was incumbent on her to believe the captain too.

"Do you want to know what we're going to do?" he asked, stroking her cheek.

"Well, I imagine it's something like investigate, find the bad guys, and save the world. Does that sound right?"

"I'd say that's pretty perceptive."

"No, I just know you. And you have a track record for certain things. It's just who you are, Kyle."

She was reminded again, as they walked back to bed, that living with someone like Kyle came with so much baggage her life would never truly be her own, and her kids wouldn't get as much of him as she wanted them to, because he was off doing all the dumb stuff heroes did. But at times like these, when a new challenge appeared on the horizon, her job was to embrace it and enjoy every minute alone with him that she had.

Because there was always that thought rolling around in the back of her mind, keeping her from truly freaking out.

Life is fragile. Grab all you can get.

He loved like he lived. She made sure he didn't feel her fear as she gave him back everything she had and then a few more sparks of magic more.

CHAPTER 14

KYLE WAS UP early, slipping out of bed before the sun was up on the horizon. He decided to let Christy and the kids sleep in, since they weren't to arrive in Puerto Vallarta until close to noon. They had signed up for a fiesta in town, so it would be a late night.

The adventures of yesterday loomed large in his head. He wanted to see if Sanouk was able to make any headway with the thumb drive he'd received from Captain Antonini.

Although Christy had tried to get all the rooms together, Sanouk and Timmons shared a room on the other side of the grand stairway. He crossed the lobby area, headed left toward the rear of the ship, and softly knocked on their door.

Sanouk appeared in the crack, his hair disheveled and his eyes very bloodshot. They had whisked him off a dance floor where he'd been partying with several girls to put him to work on their secret mission, and now Kyle felt like an idiot robbing him of a good time and waking him up so early.

"Hey, I'm sorry, Sanouk. I just wanted to see if you got anywhere with that drive."

Sanouk opened the door, revealing a room that looked like a boys' dorm hovel. It had been completely trashed with discarded and dirty clothes strewn everywhere. His stepfather, Timmons, was lying on his back and snoring up a storm, his beefy torso rising and falling in cadence with the gurgling sounds of a choking alligator. They'd kept their drapes closed, so probably weren't aware that it was going to be dawn soon. He opened the door wider to allow Kyle entry.

"No, I'm sorry. I'll come back later."

Sanouk put his finger in front of his lips and closed the door behind him, addressing Kyle in the hallway. That's when Kyle noticed he was wearing Avenger pajama bottoms.

"I worked on it until about three o'clock, and I'm dead tired. But there's a lot of stuff on that thumb drive, and I'm going to need a little bit of help. I mean, I could have downloaded like two gigs, and there's just so much I don't know where to start, Kyle."

"Okay, well, at least you got access to the ship's cargo load, correct?"

"Yeah, it's all there. I think so anyway. But man,

they have pallets coming in from every port of call. They have pallets from their previous trip that haven't even been opened yet, and then they've got fresh produce going back and forth—waste and even laundry. It's a huge undertaking to keep track of all that stuff. You would think they'd keep it all separate, right?" Sanouk had a serious frown on his face. "But it's all random and with no way to make any sense out of it. What am I looking for?"

Kyle studied the hallway as if expecting someone to greet them shortly. Then he thought of something.

"Can you search like alpha or numerically? Can you move the files at all?"

"I don't know. I could try. It's not Excel. I've never used this kind of inventory software before, but it shouldn't be too hard, I guess."

"What if you downloaded parts of it into a spreadsheet somewhere and created your own program so to speak?"

"Yeah, I could, but you know what, Kyle? I'm dead tired. And seeing all those numbers go up and down on my screen, man, I was starting to get seasick. I just think I should do it where I have more light, maybe outside when it's daytime. I was trying not to wake Timmons, so I didn't put the light on. But I'll work on it. I'm going to get an hour or two of extra sleep, if you don't mind. And then I'll see what I can do."

"No problem. We got time. And thanks, I'm glad at least you got the raw data."

"That we did. Raw as shit."

He agreed to check back with Sanouk later. "And thanks, man. I really appreciate this."

Kyle ran down five flights of stairs to the promenade level to see if the espresso stand was open. He waited about five minutes, noticing activity in the prep room. The attendant unlocked the gate, so Kyle was first in line to get a cappuccino and a pastry.

He sat in the corner where he, T.J., and Dr. Bonelli had talked the day before. Wired up and ready to go, Kyle was anxious to get enough research accomplished for Captain Antonini that he could spend more time with the family. He didn't want to be doing this all day long. He wanted to accompany them to Puerto Vallarta and attend the dinner tonight.

He thought about the captain and his past history. Kyle had some serious concerns about how he would find out about the human trafficking and not be aware of it happening on his own ship. He hoped that the man could be trusted, but Kyle really wasn't one hundred percent sure. He decided to go with his gut, which told him, this very successful and private man was being laid bare by his upcoming date with death, and with such a fast-advancing cancer, perhaps he felt he needed to rely on outside help like Kyle and the team.

Kyle hadn't had time to give Collins a call, so he decided to wake his liaison up. Besides, this was a conversation he didn't want to have in front of his children or Christy, and he didn't want a lot of strangers listening in, either.

"What the fuck, Kyle? It's six A.M." Collins was not an early riser, even though he managed a team that would check in with him at all hours of the day or night. He was not used to it, after all these years being their handler.

"Come on, Collins, I'm just keeping you healthy. And I have something kind of important, and I really need your advice."

"Okay, let me get my glasses on." Kyle could hear him rustling around. A door closed, and footsteps sounded as Collin's hiked down a hallway or climbed the stairs followed by heavy breathing. He heard the sounds of springs and figured his handler had sat on an easy chair away from his sleeping wife. "Okay. I got pen and paper, and I'm alone. So what you got."

"I happened to spot a couple of underage females here, who were being held down in the crew quarters, and they looked like they were in for some rough times, possibly kidnap or traffic victims. They both wore a gag, one had been beaten up a little bit, and they definitely weren't happy."

"And what, pray tell, were you doing down in the crew quarters? You're a married man. Are you suddenly on the prowl? Is that the kind of trouble you're talking about?"

"No, sir. I had taken Luke down there. He broke his arm, and he'd seen the ship's doctor—"

"Broke his arm? This is your little guy?"

"Yes. But that's another story."

"Spare me. Let's get to the point. So you didn't stumble upon some kind of a sex thing then."

"No, absolutely not. The door was open, and the guy was a real jerk—even tried to get the girls to deny he was hurting them. But they were really young, and I don't think they spoke English. So I made the decision to inquire about them and their welfare, and I asked the ship's doctor about it. As it turned out, the doctor is also kind of compromised, because his medical license has been suspended or not renewed in the United States. This is a violation of the terms of agreement for the cruise ship. So even though I don't think he's involved, he is definitely compromised."

"Which should not be your problem unless he's doing emergency surgery. You got Coop and T.J. They're better than any ship doc around."

"Except he had an X-ray machine."

"Gotcha. Okay, so you talked to this doctor, and what did he say?"

"He said he would look into it and speak with the captain or one of the junior officers. Then last night, I spoke with the captain, and we had a little four-way chat. I was with T.J. and Coop, and he gave me a heads-up on what he thought could be happening here with the cruise line. He thinks perhaps the cruise line, not his ship but on other ships, was engaging in some sort of illegal commerce, more specifically human trafficking. But I wouldn't rule out other stuff too. It's a pretty rough crowd here, down below."

"It usually is, which is why you have no business there, Kyle."

"Except that's where the doctor is."

"Of course, they'd be close to the drugs. Well, they get people from all over the world, often those that don't want to be found anywhere. I understand sometimes they pick up criminals or unsavories that somehow fake their credentials. It happens. The coast guard has run across several of these ships crewed by almost all convicts or ex-convicts. Just like the old British Navy. And they're not into any good stuff at all."

"So, one of the other things he said was that he wanted to make sure that his ship was not participating in any of this. He gave us a thumb drive of his cargo hold. And honest to God, Collins, I had Sanouk put it on his computer last night, and he stayed up till three.

He said there's a lot of stuff on it. But it's hard to decipher."

"Now wait a minute, Kyle. You didn't tell captain What's-his-face that you were going to investigate his ship, did you?"

"Well, I sort of—"

"Fuck me, Kyle. Don't do that to me. This is not a fucking game. I've told you this many times before. We butt out of other countries' businesses. I know he operates in the United States and he's in international waters, but you have no authority to lend your skills. I mean, it's almost like you've agreed to have the Navy help him with the trafficking issue."

"That's why I'm calling you. And here's why I think he's telling the truth and why I think it's important. Captain Antonini's wife and granddaughter were kidnapped. His wife was killed, and his granddaughter was sold into slavery. And to make matters worse, the captain has been diagnosed with terminal cancer and has probably two months to live, or so he's been told."

Collins let out a long sigh, obviously distressed with this news. "How you managed to find these things is just unreal to me. Why can't you just go on a fucking vacation with your wife and kids? Why can't you just sit back, sip margaritas and parrot drinks, and have a good time?"

"You know how it is, Chief. You did your time. It's

a dying man's wish. He lost everything that he had that was valuable. And he wants revenge. He knows I can't arrest these guys or do anything. He just wants me to check, and if we get names of some suppliers or sources or anything in Mexico or Central America or South America that State knows is into this stuff, that's a tip. That's a big lead, and somebody in the CIA or our Justice Department could go after them. I'm not going to do that, of course. I'm just here to give him more ammunition so he can get even. But we're not going to launch an invasion or anything."

"Says the guy who can't stay out of a fight. Kyle, I don't want to do another cruise takeover like before. We all nearly got busted on that one."

"It won't be. But I want you to get me some direction from the Headshed, please. Give me some instructions on what I can and cannot do. And what kinds of information should I look for. We got hundreds and hundreds of names and manifest numbers, coming from all sorts of ports of call onboarding and offloading. I just want something I can search by, something that maybe Justice or the coast guard or somebody is working on, hoping to catch, and let's see what we can do to help our guys out and help this guy too. But, no, I got all the wives here. I mean, there's fifty-three of us, and over half of them are kids. I have no intention to get into a firefight."

The silence on the other end of the line was difficult for Kyle. He knew that Collins was going to have to decide to make that phone call to Norfolk or Washington, and if he didn't want to, there wasn't anything Kyle could do. He'd have to return the thumb drive, sympathize with the captain, and stay out of it, which was probably the safest thing he could do.

But Collins considered it and told him this. "I'll make one call. I know a guy in DC. They were working on some things, and I'll ask him if it's worth pursuing. I don't have any doubt that this type of thing goes on, but it's just not what we do. And it's really not your job."

"I know that, sir. Thanks, Collins. I appreciate it."

"I can't imagine this is going over very well with Christy. She okay with you spending all this time, doing this research, running around, and finding bad guys when you're supposed to be on vacation?"

"Well, if I told you she was okay with it, you'd know I was lying. And that's part of the reason I'm calling you, because if you say no, then I've got a reason to back out. But what I'm hoping I can get from you and your friend is just a little more of a focus, something to go after. If it's a little easier to search, I might be able to do some good without getting fully involved. And at the end of the day, we're all in this thing together. I mean, it's terrible what they're doing—the drugs, the girls, all the stuff. It's dangerous. It's ruining people's lives. And it has to stop."

"Slavery has been around for centuries, and it's certainly not going to stop now. But I hear you, and I know it's coming from a good place, Kyle. I admire that. I just wish you kept your eyes a little more closed from time to time. It would make my job so much easier."

CHAPTER 15

CHRISTY FELT THE warm body of her daughter slip into bed with her. She wrapped her arms around the child, kissing the top of her head. A glance over to the bunk beds, and she determined that the boys were still asleep and decided to keep it that way. She noted that Kyle was missing.

"How are you this morning, Maggie?" she asked as she hugged her again.

"I'm cold. When is Daddy coming back?"

"I woke up and he's gone, but he should be right back. Otherwise, he would have left me a note. Sometimes he just has to walk or take a run and think about things."

Maggie nodded her head and cuddled closer to Christy.

"Are you having a good time?" she asked her daughter.

"Yes, I've met lots of new children, and the playroom has been really fun. I like it much better than being stuck with my brothers all the time."

"I can only imagine. You're a real trooper, Maggie, and I appreciate you so much."

"Mama?"

"Yes, sweety?"

"Is Daddy gone on deployment, or is he going to leave us soon?"

The question melted Christy's heart. She knew the kids worried about their father a lot more than they ever let on. She didn't like the fact that Maggie now was burdened with that concern.

"No, sweetheart. But I do wish he would be around us more. I talked to him last night, and he promised he won't be tied up much longer."

"Does everybody's daddy have to work so hard?"

"Well, everybody else's daddies do different things, honey. Some work in an office, some build houses and work outside, some are cooks, and some are teachers. You know, daddies do different things all the time. What's special about your daddy is that he works for Uncle Sam, he works for the Navy, and he has very special jobs."

"Brandon says he does secret stuff."

"Well, Maggie, it's not really secret, but it's things that you really can't talk about. You know that Daddy has asked you about this before, right?"

"Yes. I remember. I try not to. But sometimes my friends ask me."

"I'm sure they do. I have people that ask me all the time, too, especially when they find out that your daddy does special things. But the most important thing to remember is that your daddy is a hero, and he loves you very much, and even though he does really important things, he would much rather be with you. And that's the truth, Maggie."

"Do you miss him?"

Christy's eyes immediately filled with tears. She wasn't going to let Maggie see this. Waiting just long enough so her voice didn't waiver, she answered her, "I miss him very much. I wish he was with us every minute of every single day."

"Yeah, that's what I thought. I miss him too. I don't ever want him to leave us."

Christy was concerned with that comment. "Maggie, why would you say that?"

"Well, there was that girl. Remember the girl that was in my class for a while, and her daddy didn't come home? Her mommy moved away."

"Yes, I remember. He was one of the men on SEAL Team 5. And yes, there was an accident, and he did not come home. Her family went back to live with their grandmother in Kansas. That was too bad."

"I don't want that to happen to Daddy."

"He's promised me, and when you see him, you can make him promise you too."

Maggie snuggled closer again, wrapping her arms around her mother and clutching her pink rabbit in her right hand, and fell asleep.

Christy knew they were to spend time shopping and attend a Mexican fiesta this evening. But right now, she was enjoying being lazy and the warmth of her bed with her daughter at her side. She was glad the boys could sleep so easily. They'd been very active, so she was happy they were getting rest.

Through the sliding glass door, she saw the sky turning blue from pink, and she could catch just a glimpse of the top of the very calm Pacific Ocean. The ship had slowed down considerably, so Christy understood that perhaps they were navigating in shallow waters, maybe just a few miles off the coast as they prepared for their approach.

A gentle knock at the door awoke her. She hadn't realized that she'd fallen asleep. Very carefully, she extricated herself from Maggie's arms, threw a robe over her shoulders, and opened the door a crack. Cooper was standing there with his medic kit.

"Can I come in and check Luke?"

"Sure, he's still asleep, though. Do you want to come back?"

Coop glanced at the bed and asked, "Where's

Kyle?"

"He wasn't here when I woke up this morning. You know him. He's probably out for a run. I expect him back any time."

"Well, I don't want to come in unless Kyle is here. So you guys just knock on my door when you're ready, and I'll take a look and change his bandage, okay?"

"Sure thing."

Before she could close the door, she heard Kyle's familiar voice whispering down the hallway. "I thought I'd catch you going after my wife when I'm away, Coop."

"Shut the fuck up. I'm here to check on your boy, goddammit. So where the hell where you?"

"I checked with Sanouk, to see how he was doing with the thumb drive."

Christy leaned out into the doorway. "Why don't you guys come inside, so you don't wake up the whole floor?"

Cooper entered followed by Kyle, who gave Christy a big hug and kiss.

"Well, hello there, stranger," she said.

"I didn't want to wake you, and the kids were sawing logs. I decided to just go take a run then check on something with Sanouk, and I really thought I'd be back sooner."

They continued whispering until Cooper sat on the

edge of Luke's bunk bed, rolled him over, and discovered his bandage was hanging by a very ugly looking piece of tape. The wound appeared to be oozing.

"It looks fine, a little weepy, but I'm going to have to clean it, put a little Neosporin on it, and then put a fresh bandage. The next two or three days are going to be really important, so make sure he's supervised all the time, okay?"

Christy nodded. She retrieved a warm washrag from the bathroom and handed it to Coop. "Do you want me to put soap on it?"

"No, I think this is fine." He dabbed the wound with the washcloth, removing the rest of the tape and the gauze pad. He handed the pad and the washcloth back to Christy.

Luke began to stir and, when he noticed Cooper leaning over him, startled slightly. He turned his head quickly from side to side until he could see both of his parents.

"Luke, I'm just here to change your bandage, okay?"

"Okay. Am I getting better?"

"You are. How does it feel?"

"It's still a little hot, but I feel okay."

"Does it itch? Do you have an itchy sensation?" Coop asked.

"No. It just hurts a little bit. If I bump it, it really

hurts."

"Well, that's exactly what you're not going to do, right?" Kyle said to him.

Cooper reapplied the gauze pad with fresh tape after placing the Neosporin gel on the wound. He checked the splint that Dr. Bonelli had placed on him and readjusted the bandages, wrapping them slightly tighter around his forearm to protect the broken bone. He squeezed above and below where Luke had fractured the bone and asked if it hurt.

Luke shook his head. "Maybe a little."

"It's only been a couple days. We should get it X-rayed again tomorrow and see how it's doing. But kids heal very fast."

Cooper petted Luke on the head, stood, and added, "Just make sure he doesn't get it wet, okay, either of them." He gestured to the forehead and Luke's arm.

"Thanks, Coop," said Christy. "I feel much better after you've checked him out."

Cooper left quietly, and Kyle looked at Maggie snuggled in the covers, sleeping still. Brandon was still out cold. "You want to sleep a little bit more, sweetheart?"

"I'd like to spend more time with you. I know what I'd be doing if the kids weren't here." She smiled, and Kyle pulled her into his chest, kissing her. He whispered into her ear, "How about I just hold you until you fall asleep? How does that sound?"

"It sounds divine."

THEY WALKED THROUGH the streets in Puerto Vallarta in the early afternoon. This was a real city, not at all like the little village of Todos Santos or even Cabo. It was congested with traffic and noisy, and the downtown areas and plazas were filled with people going to and from work, home, or school. There were regular department stores and offices, police stations, and schools that they passed by on their bus trip from the pier to the shopping district. Christy wasn't really interested in doing any more shopping, but she thought perhaps she could find a few stores that the kids would enjoy and asked for a toy store.

Kyle walked around with Luke on his shoulders for part of the time, but when Brandon insisted that he have his turn, Kyle held him off. "You're getting kind of big, Brandon. A little too big to ride on my shoulders. You don't want to turn me into an old hunchback, do you?"

"Mom, how about you?"

"Oh, that's funny. You ask your dad, but if he won't do it, you ask me? I'm half his size."

"You used to ride on my shoulders all the time, Brandon. It's Luke's turn now. And besides, he's been injured."

They found the children's store and explored the boxes with foreign packaging, but the toys were similar to what they had back in San Diego. Maggie found a puppet of a white tiger with marble eyes. It was soft like her rabbit was, and she begged Christy to get it for her, which she did. The boys settled on Mexican police cars, complete with battery-operated flashing lights and an extremely annoying siren.

Kyle rolled his eyes when he discovered, after their purchase, how loud they were. "I can see this is going to keep me up some mornings."

As they strolled through the plaza, they came upon a flower shop. Exotic, large lilies, cactus flowers, protea, and colorful green and red foliage were stacked in big vases all around the little shop. The diminutive shop owner had pink and yellow chrysanthemums, enormous in size, nearly the size of Maggie's face.

At five o'clock, they gathered together at Senor Pedro's theater for the fiesta and the show. Christy suspected that it was going to be a pretty strong drinking crowd, so she suggested to Kyle that they find some place near the corner and not near the stage, which was in the middle of the theater. In several minutes, all the other SEAL families who had taken the tour joined them.

The meals were identical, except for the children's portions. The drinks were free if the adults drank rum punch. The children got soft drinks in cans with straws. The food was delicious, and Christy could only finish about a third of what she was given. Maggie didn't have much of an appetite for the food, but the boys and Kyle went back for seconds.

As the lights dimmed, they realized the floor show was about to begin. The owner of the restaurant and theater, Pedro, was costumed like a pirate with a big gold earring. He wore bright red lipstick, makeup that made his eyebrows look black and bushy, rouge, a swashbuckling pirate outfit complete with skull and crossbones eye patch, and a tricornered hat. He had a stuffed parrot sewn onto the shoulder of his jacket that flopped around as he spoke.

Pedro danced and laughed, prancing around the stage and even running up to people as he spoke about the events of this evening, and introduced the first act, which was a group of dancers, demonstrating an indigenous dance, from the ancient tribes of Mexico. The costumes were lavish and colorful. With the lights turned down low and their faces painted, Maggie got a little scared and turned her head into Christy's chest before climbing into her lap.

Several other dancers performed different acts, and then a pair of guitar players sang, jumped off the stage, and wandered through the audience, singing to the young women in the audience.

A fire dancer was the last act, reminding Christy of one of the Hawaiian fire dancers she had seen many summers ago, before she was married. He was extremely athletic, jumped high, tossed flaming spears into the air and caught them again, shouted, and danced to the drums. After he left the stage, the lights came on.

The program was generally a hit with the adults, yet most of the children were sleeping by time the acts were over. But everyone thought it was a good value for their money, since it included dinner and free drinks. Together as a group, they strolled through the old part of the city, walking over tiled and cobblestone streets lit by torches and listening to the sounds of traffic dying low, the occasional rooster, a scooter, or a dog barking. They met their bus at the appointed fountain, climbed aboard, and headed back to the ship. Most everybody fell asleep on the way back even though it was barely a ten-minute ride.

The bus brought them all the way to the gangway. Kyle lifted Luke in his arms, while Christy held Maggie and tugged Brandon along behind. She could tell he was feeling the regret of being the oldest child and not being able to be carried any longer.

As they neared the gangway, Kyle spotted the chief engineer, who made a point to raise his head and signal he would like to talk. With Luke still in his arms, he headed toward the engineer, Christy following close behind. With Brandon holding onto her skirts and Maggie fast asleep in her arms, she watched the engineer speak in broken English.

"You have a very nice family, Mr. Lansdowne."

"Thank you. What can I do for you, sir?"

"I understand you have had a private conversation with the captain." The engineer studied Kyle's face. The way he looked at him bothered Christy. Something dark lived in there.

"I'm not sure what you're getting at, sir," her husband answered.

"Dr. Bonelli has told me some things. He is in a very difficult situation, perhaps he told you. There is much he does not know, and I am concerned that a fine father and husband, such as yourself, would get involved in something that you may not like. So I am saying to you and to your wife, you must be very, very careful. Make sure you don't go where you do not belong."

"I'll take that as a warning, then. Is that your intent?" Kyle asked him.

"You may take it however you like. But there are many things that go on that you do not see and do not know about. Some things are better left unknown, for the health and safety of your beautiful little family. Just consider it, won't you?"

CHAPTER 16

KYLE HAD BEEN threatened before. He was used to it happening when they were on missions, overseas, in little villages or towns that were exploding, or in the middle of armed insurrections. But he had never once been threatened on a luxury cruise ship by a cruise officer while he was holding his son in his arms, standing next to his wife, his other son, and his daughter. All of the things that were the most precious to him in his life, this cretin of a man had seen. And he threatened Kyle, anyway. Not only that, but now Kyle had to deal with the fact that Christy knew about it firsthand. And that was going to upset the balance of his ordered life.

The only thing Kyle could focus on was getting his family safely onboard and reporting this to the captain. But first, he had to give Collins a call. This was an A1 emergency situation. It had escalated out of his control. He also needed to gather the men together and come up with some kind of a strategy. But first, he had to find out how far they could go, and if they were told to stand down, he wasn't sure he'd be able to.

That would be a big problem.

"Come on. Not now, Christy. We got to get on the ship quick, and I have to make some phone calls." He was speed-walking away from the officer, who stood in the shadows, his arms defiantly crossed. Christy was doing her best to catch up, and Brandon was definitely dragging behind, whining and complaining about all of it. No doubt, he sensed the tension between his parents.

"Kyle," he heard Christy sigh from behind. "Please stop for a minute. I need to talk to you."

"We have to get on the ship, right now."

"Kyle!"

He turned, knowing what he'd see, and wasn't disappointed. Christy stood still, her face filled with fear, shock, horror, and more than a little anger. She walked to him as passengers passed them by, heading to the gangway.

"Tell somebody right now. You've got to get some help."

"I will, but the safest place for us to be is on the ship. We're vulnerable here. I'm trying to get you out of here and to safety. Please understand me."

Christy searched the flock of oncoming traffic, noticing several men from Kyle's team. Danny walked with his family, Trace with Gretchen and the three girls, and Coop and Libby with their two children. She pointed to several of the men. "Tell them now. I'm waiting right here." Kyle power-walked over to Trace and then Danny. He whispered something in their ears, and pretty soon, they started notifying some of the other men that they saw in the crowd.

He returned. "We're getting the word out. The chief has seen this, too, but nothing I can do about that. Now, will you hurry up and get on the ship, Christy? I'm going to call Coronado and let them know about this. I believe we're in imminent danger. My job is to get you and everyone here to safety."

Christy ran as fast as she could, but Maggie was heavy in her arms. She shifted weight with Luke, and Kyle took Maggie while Luke wanted to walk. She encouraged both Luke and Brandon to run and keep up with her pace. Several of the other families rushed to get on the ship as well.

"I need to warn Captain Antonini, but first, I'm going to get you to the cabin. And then I'll call Collins in California. You spread the word that everyone is to stay in their cabins for the rest of tonight. I may not be able to reach everyone. I need your help."

"You got it." But she barely had time to say anything further when they reached the X-ray machines.

Christy couldn't find her onboard pass at first and held up the line for several minutes, until she finally located it in the bottom of her bag. Their family slipped through the package inspection line and ran to the elevator banks, pushing the buttons and getting up to the tenth level without waiting for anyone else to join them. Kyle tore down the hall with Maggie in his arms, opened the door to their cabin, and placed Maggie down on the bed. He shed his backpack, met Christy in the hallway, picked up Luke, and brought him to the bunk bed. Christy rushed through the doorway with Brandon. Kyle stood in front of her, placing his hands on her shoulders. He could see that she was petrified, and she looked to him for help.

"I need to get hold of the Captain Antonini first, and then I'll make my other calls. I've arranged for the men to meet me in the café, as soon as they get their families situated, and for everyone to reach someone else by text or phone call, so that everyone knows what's going on. Would you call Timmons' place and let him and Sanouk know?"

"They didn't go to town with us today?" Christy asked.

"No, Sanouk had a job to do for me, and he opted to stay back. And I think they had a little too much to drink last night and needed the rest as well."

"So I'm to stay here with the kids then, is that

right?"

"Yes, please. Get your lists out and start contacting people. We have to make sure everyone is safely on board and understands what just occurred." He grabbed her in his arms and, with all of the power and urgency he could muster, squeezed her hard and whispered to her ear, "Please try to stay calm. Please keep the kids calm. I know it's a lot to ask of you, but there's a lot riding on it, and I don't want to further stress you, but it's the truth. I promise you I'm going to get us out of this somehow, but please help me by keeping everybody calm."

"I've got the list I prepared with everyone's cell and text message number. I'll get working on the ones I didn't see today. I'm not even sure everyone went to town today. I don't think T.J. and Shannon did. At least, I didn't see them. What about Lizzie and Jameson?"

Kyle trying to recall everyone he saw in town, and he could not place Jameson, Lizzie, Shannon or T.J. "Hon, I gotta go. Would you contact the men please and tell them to meet at the cafe in a half an hour?"

Christy nodded her head.

Kyle squeezed her again, kissed her on the side of the cheek, and began to leave the room when he remembered to lean down and give Maggie, Luke, and Brandon a hug.

"Daddy, are you leaving to go to work?" Maggie asked.

"Something very important has come up. Luke, you remember the bad man?"

Luke nodded his head quickly.

"Your daddy has to do something, but I promise you that I am going to protect you. You stay with your mother, you do everything she says, and no arguing about it. Do we understand each other?"

All three of the kids reflected back to him the gravity of the situation. Little Maggie's lower lip began to quiver. He reached out and touched her cheek. "Maggie, I promise you it's going to be okay."

Maggie ran to her mother. Christy sat with her on the bed and instructed the boys to get their pajamas on.

"I'll be back as soon as I can. It'll be probably an hour, and please have them meet me there, okay?"

"You got it. Be careful. Be safe. And please come back."

All the way down the hallway and through the lobby of the grand staircase, those last words of Christy's hooked his heart. He felt like a fool for having placed them in such a dangerous position. If he hadn't brought up what he had seen in the room the other morning, none of this might've happened. But now he had created an enemy, and he didn't know how many of the enemy there were. But he had to warn the captain, and then he had to get on the phone with Collins.

Instead of waiting for the elevator, he ran up the two flights until he got to the bridge level. He leapt up the five steps and knocked on the bridge door. One of the junior officers answered.

"I need to speak to Captain Antonini. It's very urgent."

"He's not here. He went to town today. He's not returned."

"Does he have a cell phone?"

The junior officer looked puzzled and frowned, checking with a Antonini's second-in-command, who shook his head. "Excuse me, but I'm not allowed to give you that information."

Kyle nearly grabbed him by the collar to shake some sense into the young officer, but he resisted the urge. "I said it's a matter of life and death. I need to speak to the captain *now*. Would you call him please for me and have him call my number?"

The officer looked beyond Kyle and then whispered, "Come inside for a minute." Kyle stepped into the bridge and found only two other officers present. Since the ship was tied in port, they were operating on a skeleton crew, readying the ship for departure. The junior officer dialed a phone on the ship's comm and began speaking in Italian.

"What is your number please, sir?" he asked Kyle.

Kyle shouted his phone number with the area code.

The call was disconnected. "He says he will call you in five minutes."

"Thank you." Kyle was going to run downstairs but turned and asked one more question. "Is he on the ship or is he still on shore?"

"He has just boarded the ship."

Somewhat relieved, Kyle practically flew off of the bridge, barely touching the six steps, ran down the stairway several floors until he got to Deck Five, the promenade. He briskly dodged passengers who were ogling closed stores and helping themselves to ice cream and candies, but the shops themselves would remain closed until they got back out to sea. He smelled the coffee and found Trace, Coop, T.J., and Danny Begay sitting in the corner where he and T.J. had interviewed the doctor before. All four of the men looked worried.

"What the fuck is going on, Kyle?" asked Danny.

"T.J., glad to see you."

"Trace told me. Others are coming, Kyle."

"Good. You remember the engineer we met at the captain's reception?" The men nodded their heads.

"He threatened me. He threatened my family. He told us basically to butt out of their little scheme. Up until this point, I would have thought that there was no involvement or nefarious activities going on in the ship, but with the engineer's attitude and the threat that he posed, now I know something is really wrong. And I fear, we're all in danger."

"What do you want us to do, to tell the others? Do we have a plan?" asked Cooper.

"Well, that's next on my list. I'm going to give Collins a follow-up call from this morning. I'm sure as hell hoping he'll have some direction. But in the meantime, we have to keep everyone safe in their rooms. No exception."

Before he could continue, Captain Antonini rang.

"What is this urgent matter? Do you have news for me?" the Captain asked over the phone.

"Your chief engineer? He threatened me tonight. He knows that I spoke to you, and he threatened me."

"But he knows nothing of our conversation, unless someone from the bridge—"

"He knows *something*, Captain. And he told me that I was risking my family's life if I continue to stick my nose where it was not wanted. I need to tell you that I think this man is dangerous, and you need to watch your back."

"I thank you for this. This confirms my suspicions, then. What about the other matters we discussed?"

"That's going to be my next call. I'll let you know once I know."

Kyle hung up the phone and dialed Collins. He was forced to leave a voicemail, which irritated him. Glancing at the faces of the other men in front of him, he decided to dial again and left another message.

"Dammit."

Several of the other SEALs showed up, even Timmons.

"How is Sanouk coming with his work?" asked Kyle.

"I've been trying to help him work on the files a little bit. There's a lot there, Kyle. Some of the stuff is encrypted, and we don't have a way to break in. I sure do wish we had some fucking idea who we're looking for. It would be so much easier." Timmons was obedient but irritated. Kyle didn't blame him one bit.

"I'm on it. Waiting for Collins now, but he has a source who might be able to help."

Just then his phone rang. Before Kyle could speak, Collins shouted in his ear.

"Okay, Kyle, you stepped on a hornet's nest. The Headshed is extremely interested in your manifest. Is there a way that it can be transmitted to them in Virginia?"

"God, I didn't think of it, Collins. It never occurred to me to even offer that. Sanouk has been playing with it all day. I'll see if he can do that, but in the meantime, something new has happened. The chief engineer has threatened me—told me with my kids in my arms, standing next to Christy, that I was endangering my family if I didn't stop poking my nose in his business, as he called it. This man knows that we're launching something, and he's come out and actively threatened me."

"He's the engineer, an officer?"

"Yes, he is. He runs the crew downstairs. I have informed the captain, and I'm just waiting for instructions from you."

"Where are the wives and kids?"

"They're all waiting in their rooms. Collins, you got to get me some backup, some help here. I don't know how many of them there are, but they're planning something. And most of us are not armed."

"I got you. Well, my friend back in DC told me there is one company that has been transporting drugs and arms from Central America, Venezuela, Mexico, and parts of North America. It's called XFR or XFR Corp or something like that on the manifest. You see if you have any pallets from that particular company on your ship. We would be very, very interested in it if so. It might enable me to get you some Naval back up."

"Okay. XFR. Let me go get Sanouk and see if I can download this to you. Give me an IP address to send it to."

Collins gave Kyle an encrypted address with the

warning, "You may not have the bandwidth to send it. I don't know what kind of computer Sanouk has. Maybe you could use the captain's computer?"

"I'm running out of time. I will ask, though. So we'll try to get this to you, and then I'll call you back with the information on the manifest? And wait? Is that what we're supposed to do? I got a lot of people depending on me, sir."

"Goddammit, Kyle, be safe. If XFR is involved, my buddy in DC says that they are ruthless and will stop at nothing. So don't take any chances. You be careful."

When Kyle hung up, Timmons tapped him on the chest. Nodding, he told Kyle, "I saw several manifest lists, a ton of stuff from XFR, Kyle. This ship is loaded with their crap."

"Well, gentlemen, I think it's safe to say that this has officially stopped being a vacation. We are on a full-on, no-holds-barred mission. Problem is, we have the wives and kids and two thousand other innocent passengers on this ship. I'm going to hope that our Navy sees fit to give us a little hand. But in the meantime, we have to keep our eyes and ears open and be ready for anything. Keep your family together, stay in your rooms as much as possible, and we'll sort this out somehow. I will feel better about all this once we leave port. Then we have two days at sea. I hope to God in that period of time we can manage to come to some resolution, but a lot of it depends on what we do next. So stay with your wives and kids."

"How are we going to get food for everyone? How are we going to keep the kids holed up in our rooms for two days?" asked Danny.

"I think staying in their cabins is the safest place to be."

"You got it. I'll await further orders, then." Danny, Trace, and T.J. left.

Kyle handed the paper with the IP address on it to Timmons. "You give Sanouk this and tell him to try to upload the whole file to this email address. You call me if he has any trouble whatsoever."

"Will do, Kyle. You can count on it."

CHAPTER 17

L IBBY BROUGHT GILLIAN and Will over to Christy's room. The TV partially occupied the kids after Christy confiscated their noisy Mexican police cars.

"How are you doing, Libby?"

"I've only got two. You've got—what?—nearly fifty?"

"Don't remind me." She wished she'd never planned the trip but didn't want to express it.

"We have to get a food chain going somehow. Need to make plans to get everyone milk, especially for the babies. We've not brought a lot of stuff into these tiny rooms because we could get it at the buffets, but we have to take turns and go out."

Libby made a good point.

"I'll see what Kyle says. Maybe the guys can do it. I think we're going to have to combine rooms, like we did here. It's too hard when they're separated all over the floor. If we keep the kids and moms together, then the guys can plan the defense. I just hope Kyle got to the captain and to Collins."

"Funny how everyone wants privacy, and then when there's danger, everyone wants to be together. The way the ship is set up, even the Presidential Suites aren't big enough for a large gathering. Not on this ship, anyway." Libby retrieved a washcloth from the bathroom, wet it down, and placed it at the back of her neck. "You want one, Christy?"

"I'm good."

They both looked at the five children. Luke and Maggie were passed out on the bottom bunk. Gillian was on the upper bunk with Will and Brandon. No one was paying attention to the TV, so Christy turned it off.

"Lie down, why don't you, Christy? I'm sure he'll be back soon," said Libby.

"Thanks. I think I will. I got up so early this morning. With all the walking we did, it's been a really long day. I'm completely bushed."

"You go ahead and fall asleep if you need to. I'll stay and watch the kids. You could use my room, if you wanted to."

"No, I promised him I wouldn't go anywhere by myself."

Just then, Kyle walked through the door.

"Have I died and gone to Heaven? I've got two beautiful wives and now five kids."

"Funny. We don't speak about that 'D' word, remember?" reminded Christy. "So what's the plan, Stan?"

"I talked to Collins. There might be some interest in the ship's manifest logs after all. Sanouk is trying to upload them to him now. Looks like we have a match to some very bad dudes they've been trying to catch red-handed. Fingers crossed."

Just then, the ship's motors came roaring back to life, and the hunt back to the waters of the Pacific and the safety of the US was on. It did make Christy feel some hope.

"Did you find the captain?" Libby asked.

"I did. I warned him about his chief engineer. Since then, we've learned that this boat is literally riddled with pallets from one of the contraband providers from Central America."

"So, Kyle, Libby and I were talking, and we need to come up with a strategy to get food to the rooms, especially milk for the babies. We're going to have to make a schedule, have people go in shifts. Should I start making a plan?"

"Maybe break the rooms down into blocks? One pair can go out for needed food for their own group? Something like that?"

"That would work," said Christy. "I've got the floorplan of Deck 10 and the rooms marked. We could just break them down in groups of three or four rooms each? We've got four mothers with babies. They should come first, don't you think?"

"I agree," Kyle said.

While Christy and Libby worked on their rooming plan, Kyle got a call.

"Good job. All of it? You got the whole manifest sent?"

Christy and Libby smiled to each other. This was obviously good news.

"Okay, I'll see what he wants to do next. You stand by. And, Timmons, while he's on the computer, might we be able to convince you to help get some food for the little ones? There should be soft drinks, milk, maybe some fruit you could pick up at the midnight buffet. You game? Awesome! Thanks, man."

He hung up and grinned from ear to ear. "Sanouk got the whole thing sent out. God, I love that kid."

"And you got Timmons getting milk and stuff. Should I call Kate, Julie, Brandy, and Shannon to let them know?"

"Good idea," said Kyle. He plugged his phone into the charger beside the bed.

"And I'll help. You take Julie and Kate. I'll call the other two," added Libby.

"I'm calling San Diego in the hallway. Be back in a sec," said Kyle.

Christy got Julie on the first ring. "Hey, sweetheart, just letting you know we're sending out for some fruit and milk for the babies, snacks for whatever until morning. Do you need anything else?"

"Thanks, I was just going to send Luke out for some milk and some waters for me. Who's going?"

"Timmons. I'll get him to drop it by your room, and I'll make sure he brings water, okay?"

"Thanks so much. Do we know what the plan is yet?"

"Tonight, we're waiting for instructions. We might be getting help, but it's not official. Remember, stay in your room. Or you could combine the kids if you want, might give you some time alone for nursing?"

"They're crashed right now. So is Luke. I'm going to let sleeping dogs lie, if you know what I mean."

Christy heard Libby connect with Shannon then refocused back on her call. "Gotcha. Well, let me know if you need anything else, and watch for that knock on the door."

She texted Timmons to add yogurt and waters to the order. Too late, she realized they should have sent someone else with him. Next, she dialed Kate.

"Hey, Christy."

The noise in the background was overpowering. It sounded like they were having a pillow fight.

"What's going on?"

"Oh, we have a full house. Ginger wasn't feeling well, so Jake's lying down with her while we have Jasmine and Jennifer over here, along with Angela, Gretchen's youngest. The three girls are spoiling Grady something fierce. He's never had so many playmates who laugh at everything he does. The guys are out on the balcony having a cigar."

"Sounds good. Listen, I'm sending Timmons out to get some milk for the babies, some yogurts, and fruit from the buffet tonight. Do you need anything else? Water or diapers?"

"Waters would be good. I'm stocked on diapers. But I've got the milk covered. Rebecca and Clover left a few minutes ago to go get us some, but thanks."

"They what?" Christy's expression and tone caught Libby's ear.

"They went to get milk from the buffet. I think they wanted some frozen yogurt too. You know how girls are."

"Did someone go with them?"

"Gretchen approved it. She offered, but the girls jumped at the chance. Clover's sixteen, Christy. They'll be fine," Kate answered.

"But that wasn't the plan. We're supposed to keep all the kids together in the rooms, Kate."

"I'm sorry. Well, they'll be right back."

"So they went to the buffet. You're sure they went

there?"

"Yes, that's what they said."

Christy was flabbergasted she hadn't gotten the message. Gretchen was Kate's older sister. "I'm going to have Timmons look for them and escort them back to their room. No more streaking out, Kate. We have to follow the procedure."

"I'm sorry. I thought because Clover is old enough to drive, to babysit, she'd be considered almost an adult."

Christy was concerned there were too many loose ends and too many options. Kyle wouldn't be pleased Tyler and Trace hadn't stopped it.

"Okay. Let me know when they get back, okay?"

"Sure thing. You get some rest now, Christy. For tomorrow."

"I will," she lied.

The truth was, she'd worry about the two girls until she heard they were back in the cabin, safe.

Libby was done with her two calls. "What's wrong?" she asked.

"Kate and Gretchen let Gretchen's oldest two girls out to get some milk."

"Oh dear."

"I better get hold of Timmons and have him bring them back to their room."

She texted the former Senior Chief. The answer she

got back was chilling.

'*I'm up here now, and I don't see either one of the girls,*' he texted.

"I gotta get Kyle." Christy ran to the door and found him on his way in.

"What's up?"

"I can't believe it, but they let Rebecca and Clover out to get some milk and things for Kate. I just texted Timmons, who's at the buffet now, and there's no sign of them."

"I'm praying they're on their way back now and just missed each other. I'll go down and look for them. No one else leave this place, okay?"

About ten minutes later, he came back, crestfallen. His face was white as a sheet.

"Christy, we better start calling all the rooms again. We can't find the girls anywhere."

CHAPTER 18

KYLE REQUESTED EVERYONE get their families in bed and combine the wives and kids as best they could, but make it a reasonable situation, so the ladies and the kids could get some rest. He instructed the men to meet him in Timmons' and Sanouk's cabin.

Before the meeting, he wanted to touch base with two people. First, he needed to update Collins, and then he needed to talk to the captain. He was pretty sure he could count on the captain to help him out. But he was worried for the captain's safety as well. Collins was so far away, and he didn't figure there were any Coast Guard or Navy ships nearby, so even though he'd hoped they could get some backup, the reality was, after he thought about it, they were on their own with their families, their kids, and two thousand other innocents. It didn't take very many bad guys to do something horrible, and Kyle knew that the Navy wouldn't want him to engage full-on like they had on the cruise ten years ago when they stopped a terrorist attack.

"So I hope you have some good news for me, Collins, 'cause I got some real bad news for you."

"You first," Chief Collins mumbled.

"Rebecca and Clover are missing. Those are Trace and Gretchen's—"

"I know who they are. And that's a damn shame. Of course, you've done all the checking you can."

"Well, we're running out of options. We've got the wives and kids here, and we can't leave 'em for very long to go searching all over the goddamn ship. There are twelve decks. There's over one thousand crew and two thousand other passengers. I mean, it's just an impossibility. You've got the cargo hold, engine rooms, the theaters, the restaurants, the lifeboats—I mean, they could be anywhere. And I'm scared, Collins. For the first time, I'm really scared."

"Okay, hold on a bit, Kyle. Let's be clear here. I'm not sure they're going to allow us to bring in a team, but let me ask you, did anybody bring any weapons with them? I know you're not supposed to, but it wouldn't be the first time."

"Chief, as far as I know, we got some knives, and I know we got one slingshot. I am not packing, and I usually do. But I didn't this time, 'cause I didn't want to have any trouble with, you know, the trouble we had the last time we were in Mexico."

Collins sighed. "Then here's the thing. If I can get permission to send a squad out to you, it's got to be a rescue. In other words, this can't be something where the girls just wandered off, and I can't deploy Navy or Coast Guard assets without being sure."

"Does that mean we have to see that they are slaughtered? Isn't kidnapping enough?"

"What I'm saying is, I just can't ask them to authorize an operation with just the disappearance of two girls and the veiled threats from an engineer. You see what I mean?"

"I have one hundred percent certainty that something is about to drop. They're not afraid of anything. Something's up. I can feel it."

"Oh, great. And that's supposed to be enough? You know I can't do that. But I'm willing to try. If I send assets out there, they're going to need permission from the captain to board. It's an Italian line, they're on international waters, and we don't yet have definitive proof of a crime, although it's very likely. And yes, that ship's manifest is helping, but we don't have proof. So here's what you do. You make sure nothing happens to that captain, and if it does, you make sure you have control of the second-in-command. Because if I don't get the approval, we cannot board. And I can't start an international incident without some protection from the State Department. It shouldn't be this way, but if your captain requests it, that holds more weight than if you do. He's in charge of everyone on board. He has the authority to determine what's needed."

"Okay, I got it. Let me see what I can do, and as we're looking for the girls, perhaps we find some contraband here? Would that help?"

"Shit, I don't know. I mean you know better than I do at this point. Just go out there and shake some tree branches and see what falls. They're not supposed to be armed on those cruise lines, but I've been told that sometimes they keep a stash somewhere, and the captain would probably know that, unless this is a planned mutiny and coup in waters. And then all bets are off. But if you're tight with him, at this point, that's your best bet, Kyle."

"Right. I'm going to meet with the guys now, and I will report back as soon as I have something. And if you've got anybody coming, please let me know."

Kyle checked his surroundings before he gave Captain Antonini a call. He waved at several of the team members who passed him on their way to the meeting.

"You still around, Captain?"

"I am. So what's the situation at this point?"

"Captain, I'm afraid the situation has escalated. We are missing two of our girls. We have a twelve-year-old and a sixteen-year-old that went upstairs to get food for their mother, the baby, and some of the other kids here and never returned. I'm going to need your help with this. I've asked my liaison back in California, and they're really too far away from anything to get any assets here right away. Our main concern is finding those girls."

"Are you sure they haven't just wandered off?"

"No, but we've traced everywhere they should be, and they aren't anywhere to be found. It would be unlike them to wander off, because they were getting milk for a couple of babies who need it. I just don't think, based on how responsible they are, that happened. I'm starting to fear that they've come into harm's way."

"You realize, I've not been told about anything like this. Most of my men, I do trust."

"I understand that. So someone's gone rogue. I have to ask you something very difficult, but by any chance, do you carry any firepower?"

"As you know, it's a violation of our charter. The punishment is severe. I would lose my position and probably go to prison. As a rule, we don't, but I do have a revolver, and I believe there is one up at the comm, something I had installed in a compartment there when we had one of our ships attacked earlier in the year. But this is between you and me, and there would be no physical way I could get it to you without someone seeing it."

"We are tasked with trying to find these girls, but I don't want to run around the ship armed. That's not what I'm talking about. Do you know anyone else of the crew who is carrying a weapon?"

"Not that I know of. Again, it would be a violation."

"We are going to need access to places that normally a passenger wouldn't go. I want to look everywhere. I want to look for them in the kitchen, in your storerooms, downstairs, maybe even in the crew quarters, and I realize this is a huge imposition, but I have to find these girls. Otherwise, all hell is going to break loose. And I don't think I can stop my guys from getting crazy. They're men of action, Captain, and not likely to want to sit around while those girls could be in danger. I don't want to panic the other passengers, either. So, the sooner we find them, the better."

"Understood. Perhaps I can help you there, since the purser has a master key to all the units, and the second set is in my office. I could provide you with the master key, which would probably mean the end of my career, but as we have discussed this before, that's not really the issue, is it?"

"At this point, Captain, that would be correct."

"I feel it is imperative that we are not seen together, and so I will try to get you this passkey if you'll give me a cabin number where it can be delivered to."

"I would prefer not to do it that way. Let me take the risk, Captain. I do not want to trust anyone else with our only vehicle to enable us to quickly search for those girls."

"Very well. I will bring my revolver and meet you in the theater. Only the wait staffs and cleaning crews should be there, since no shows are functioning this evening. If you follow the aisle to the left of stage, there is a small room we use for live artists. It is usually locked. I will meet you in that room. I will make sure that we do the transfer in private there."

"Thank you, sir. Hopefully, this will avoid any un-necessary bloodshed. Have you had any communication with your chief?"

"As a matter of fact, Mr. Lansdowne, my chief did not make it back on the ship. Also of concern to me is that I have not been able to reach Dr. Bonelli. I have reported the disappearances to my company via electronic means. They may require that I stop, pull into port at Cabo, and make a formal report. I would like to avoid this."

"Any idea where he went?"

"I saw him near the gangway as I entered the ship. No one seems to know where he disappeared to. But I have had to use his second-in-command, who is most familiar with his job. Not to worry, everything below will be taken care of, but I am not going to inform anyone on the bridge or anyone downstairs what you suspect about the girls."

"Thank you, sir. I will see you in a few minutes. Give me about twenty to speak with my men."

"Very well."

"Oh, and I forgot. My liaison says that they will need your permission to board."

"They will have it. Let's hope it doesn't come to that."

Kyle jogged to the end of the hall on the opposite side of the ship, to the room shared by Sanouk and Timmons. Upon opening the door, he observed one tiny room filled with about a dozen huge SEALs, plus Sanouk and Timmons. There was scarcely any room to turn around, let alone find a seat, so Kyle remained standing.

"Trace, my heart goes out to you. I can't imagine what Gretchen's going through right now, but we're going to get them back."

"We have to."

"I agree. Now, is there any chance that Clover and Rebecca could be wandering off somewhere, meeting up with someone their age, or just not paying attention to what they were supposed to do?"

"No way, Kyle," Trace's gravelly voice muttered. "You know that the girls have run into this before, and

Gretchen is extremely worried about the additional trauma. But with everything we've been looking into here, someone has taken them. The only good news is we're at sea, and I don't think there are any ships nearby nor have they had the opportunity to offload them somewhere. I'm going to search every fucking inch of this ship until I find them."

The grunts and whispers of support were loud. Kyle knew that every man on the team would do his utmost to help find those girls.

"Here's what I got. We can't all go searching, since we need teams protecting the women and children. We also need people out there who won't be recognized scouting around and watching for some kind of unusual activity. Sort of a look-out."

There was general agreement on this.

"Did anyone bring a weapon?"

Danny raised his hand and then produced the slingshot he had taken from Ali. "This is all I got, Kyle."

"I got a Ka-Bar," said T.J. Several others confirmed that they also brought knives.

"Anybody bring any firepower?"

No one spoke up. At last, Timmons burst out, "Fuck it, guys. I brought my SIG."

Timmons suddenly became the hero of the moment.

"I'm going to meet with the captain in a few minutes. I think he will give me his sidearm. He has a passkey, and I would suggest that a team of three go downstairs and start searching the crew quarters quickly and quietly. Try not to draw attention to yourselves. I also think I need two or three guys to start wandering through the cargo area. We're probably going to need a little distraction, maybe a few things can come undone. We can cause a little havoc without making too much of a mess?"

Several of the men started laughing, chuckling to themselves.

"I'm just thinking it would be a distraction so that the room searches get overlooked for a while," Kyle continued.

Trace raised his hand and began. "Kyle, I'd like to stay here with Gretchen and Kate, but I won't be able to live with myself if I don't find those girls."

"Understood. You stay with them. We'll need a couple more as well."

"If we haven't already, we need to combine the rooms so that we can easily keep an eye on them. It makes me really nervous when we've got eleven separate staterooms, and they're not all next to each other, not even on the same side of the ship."

"I totally agree, Trace. Who's going to help set that up?"

Jason and Jameson raised their hands. Jameson started, "Since Lizzie's pregnant, I feel I should stay with her and be her moral support, as well as help protect the others. Christy probably has a really good handle on where they should go, so I would leave it up to her. But I think you'll want them all in like three or four rooms max, instead of spread all over the place. What do you think?"

"Yeah, that's an excellent idea. I think four, plus this one for Timmons and Sanouk. Hopefully, we can have one room that's a quiet room, for people who need that. I'd like to think that the kids could sleep. If they're all together in one room, they'll not do it. Maybe two rooms for the kids, boys and girls?"

Jason spoke up next, "I think we can handle that, Kyle. And Christy, like Jameson said, she's probably already starting to work that out now anyway."

"Okay, so I got Jameson and Jason watching the women. We probably need somebody else there, too. Tyler, how about you?"

"Sure."

"Okay, that leaves Jake, Trace, Fredo, we've got Coop, Tucker, T.J., and Danny. I think I'll take the passkey and work with two of you. You know, Fredo, I think you're pretty good at making messes, so you take the rest and start doing your thing."

People laughed again.

"But I have no explosives. I don't know what I can fashion, but we'll think of something."

"I'll give you a hand there, Fredo. Maybe I can help you rig something. We can make something look like an accident," said Coop.

"I like that combination. These guys are legends for some of the mayhem they've caused in the past, right?" said Kyle.

Coop gave him a salute in return.

"Okay, so I think we got our teams set up and our jobs outlined. Fredo, you take your guys downstairs and start creating mayhem. I'm going to go meet with captain. I think I need somebody to come with me—Tucker or T.J., one of you. I just don't want to go alone in case this is an ambush."

T.J. raised his hand.

"The rest of you, head back to the rooms and help move the kids."

The meeting being over, Kyle came back to his room and let Libby and Christy know what the plan was. "We're going to need to organize into four rooms, and since we have these four rooms in a row, I think they should be over here. Christy, you work with Tyler, Jameson, and Jason to get everybody situated where they're comfortable, and I think we need to combine the kids as much as we can, but make sure the little ones get their rest and the big ones don't keep everybody awake."

Christy nodded, solemnly. "Kyle, I'd like to go see Gretchen, if I could. Kate says she's a mess. Is it safe to give her something that help her sleep?"

"I have something I can give her," said T.J.

"So you go down there and explain to the ladies what's going on. Libby, if I could ask you to stay here, we're going to be bringing kids in. If there's anything else you guys need, I can send Sanouk or Timmons to go run an errand, since they've volunteered to keep an eye up for us. I don't think they're known as being part of our team."

"That's a good idea. Of course, I will help anyway I can. These guys are not doing too bad," said Libby. "The little ones are sleeping. The three on top were playing on a Game Boy but are asleep now."

"Okay then, T.J., we're off. Thanks, Christy."

She gave him a soft kiss good-bye.

Kyle and T.J. walked casually as if they were examining places to hang out, grab a drink or a coffee, and spend a little time together. The passengers were starting to thin out and head back to their rooms, but the casino was still going strong, and several of the nightclubs were going to be operating for another couple of hours. Kyle scanned for the presence of officers or crew members that looked out of place. He didn't notice anything.

After they completed the run through the promenade on Deck 5, they walked through the double theater doors. The room had been cleared of drinks and napkins, piled up in the corner on large trays. Two young busboys were loading the trays onto plastic dollies to take to the kitchen. Kyle and T.J. walked down the side aisle of the theater, headed up the stage steps on the right, and went behind. They found a back way to go behind an interior curtain, crossing over the stage behind it, and came out on the other side. The busboys had left, so the road was clear to climb the stairs to the instrument room. Kyle turned the handle on the door and found it locked.

They heard movement inside, the door opened, and Captain Antonini greeted them, closing the door behind him. Instrument lights on a desk that featured microphones and sound equipment lit the room up with an eerie greenish glow. Captain Antonini took out the white pass card and handed it to Kyle. Then he retrieved the revolver.

"Captain, I'm going to need you to stay in touch with me, and perhaps, we should have some kind of code for if you're in danger somewhere and you need some protection, because you're all alone here. I don't know how many of your people you trust completely, but we're here for you. It's going to be very important that you be available in case they need permission to come aboard. I'm hoping it won't come to that."

Captain Antonini smiled. He placed his hand on Kyle's shoulder. "I have many regrets, Kyle. Some of them you know about. I wish that in my career as a naval officer I had a fine man like you, like all of you," he said as he nodded to T.J. "If it comes to that, and I'm all alone and in danger, I have no fear of dying, my son. It will be already too late. No code will save me."

"But we could—"

"Go find the girls. When the time comes, I'll give my permission to board."

"Thank you, sir."

"I wish I'd had fine men like you when I was serving. *Thank you*, from the bottom of my heart."

CHAPTER 19

CHRISTY AND LIBBY weighed whether to move everyone out tonight or let them sleep. They decided, with the help of the men, to move the children, which would free them to go on their search. When Kyle returned, he agreed with the plan.

They put the older boys in Christy and Kyle's room where they had the bunkbeds, plus the room was slightly larger, and it had a much larger balcony. They quietly collected clothes and backpacks, stacking them in the corner, and pulled out extra pillows and blankets harvested from other rooms to more or less make it a mattress room. Gillian, who had fallen asleep, was carried back to the room next door where her things were, while several of the older boys were brought in from various other cabins and laid down.

Remarkably, nobody objected or woke up, but Christy knew it was only a matter of time before the boys would make this room a complete terror fort. She vowed to try to get some sleep, at least a couple of hours, at least. Since Luci had two boys in this room as well, she agreed to stay with Christy and help mind the bedlam that was sure to follow.

Then the job of congregating the eight older girls to Libby and Coop's room began, watched by Libby, Ginger, and Gretchen. Ginger had brought along a small satchel of books for the girls to read, which would come in handy in the morning.

Most of the girls were awake but soon snuggled down together, happy to be having a "sleepover" together.

In Fredo and Mia's room, they put the toddlers, since they had their own four-year-old twins. Jameson's Sarah, Tyler and Kate's three-year-old Grady, Amy Paulson, and Magnus Talbot were placed in there, along with Chester until he refused to leave his mother at the last minute. Luci took him with the older boys. Lizzie, although pregnant, agreed to stay behind and help Mia with that active bunch.

The fourth room, which had been Trace and Gretchen's, was reserved for the four nursing babies and their moms. It was to become the quiet room in case there was going to be a major time out—either the parents or the children.

Timmons brought more milk, yogurts, and some cereal for breakfast, along with some fresh fruit and drinks. He and Sanouk agreed to take turns wandering the decks, including the clubs, the casino, and lobbies, just in case something popped up that caught their eye.

That also afforded them a perfect vantage spot to give regular reports to Kyle without waking the ladies.

"Should one of you take my piece?" he asked Kyle.

"Leave it here. I've got the captain's Luger, but I hesitate to use it. Besides, we got Danny's sling shot. We'll improvise, just in case we have to use something."

He said good-bye to Christy. "You call me if anything at all seems funny. But I know Jameson and Jason will take great care of you guys.

"Put the 'Do Not Disturb' signs on the rooms on your way out. I've already told the cabin boys not to bother us until noon," Christy reminded him.

"Good thinking."

"Where will you look first?" she asked.

"Downstairs in the crew quarters, but we're splitting up to cover everything."

"And the lifeboats."

He smiled, his eyes twinkling as he showed some spark for her. "How could I ever forget those?"

They kissed one last time, and then he added, "Keep looking out at the sea. If someone else pulls up alongside us, I don't want to be caught off guard."

"Will do. Where will the captain be?"

"He told me he'd be on the Bridge the whole time."

"You'll find them. I know you will."

"I think we will too. Not sure they'll expect we've got a passkey. But they better not be harmed. That's what I'm worried about the most. Say a prayer for me,

Christy."

"Always."

He leaned forward to give a wave to Libby, but she'd already fallen asleep.

She stared at the door long after he was gone. With all the sleeping children, the room was getting warm already, but she elected not to put on the air for fear of waking them all. She really needed to rest, but her mind was working overtime. Beyond tired, due to all the activities of the day and the stress of what they were trying to accomplish, she continued to stare out the window at the white caps outside caused by the movement of the ship. Like a zombie, she sat, unblinking, trying to think about what she'd do when she got home to San Diego.

She'd had enough excitement, but she wasn't complaining. It was just the way it was. Things were always a little bit out of her control. She wanted to putter in the garden and play around with rearranging the patio. Maybe she'd sort through the kids' toys and repurpose some of them elsewhere. Anything that was normal.

But it comforted her to know that these men were good at what they did and were not afraid to use force, if necessary, to get the girls to safety.

They just had to find out who had them, first.

CHAPTER 20

J AKE, DANNY, AND Trace were sent to search the dining areas, the casino, try to get inside the customer service desk offices, and the kitchen. Fredo and Coop went directly down to the cargo storage area on Deck 2 in one elevator, and Tucker, T.J., and Kyle went down in the another.

The area was nearly abandoned, so Kyle asked Tucker to go see if he could figure out how to open the cargo door without alerting the Bridge.

"Don't open it yet, because I think it has an alarm, but see if you can do it manually. I think there's a way," he added.

T.J. and Kyle did a loop around one pod of rooms, doubling back when they found one of the cabin boys doing laundry. On the opposite side and with no one visible in the hallway, Kyle pressed the key against the magnetic strip and quietly opened the door, let in T.J., and then quickly closed it behind him. Then he opened the next room, this time checking out a group of Asian men playing cards around a table with no evidence of the girls.

"Excuse me. Your door was ajar. I got the wrong room."

The men resumed their game, and Kyle left.

In the hallway, T.J. reported everyone was asleep. They followed this pattern then moved to the other side and began working those rooms beyond the medical office, without luck. They even checked Dr. Bonelli's patient room and office behind with no results.

"I'm lifting a few more pads for Luke and some surgical tape," whispered T.J.

They avoided the area around the laundry, because several men walked back and forth, carrying folded linens to a walk-in closet at the end of the hall. But T.J. did a quick check of the large laundry baskets and searched the supply cabinet and found no evidence of the girls.

Just then, they heard an enormous clanging noise as if someone had dumped a bucket of bolts on the steel plank floor. And then several large, plastic containers of what looked like potato salad rolled past the hallway.

Kyle checked around the corner and saw that Cooper had stabbed several large plastic vats of cooking oil, which added to the mess. His hands and pants were covered in a white powdery substance. He made a slice in the plastic wrap holding paper towel and napkin packages on a huge pallet, which released them to cover the area, soaking up the oil and creating wet hazard.

Fredo and Coop joined them.

"What's all over your pants?"

Coop held up his camera, showing sliced flour bags draining out on the floor. "And check out the manifest label."

Kyle read, "XFR Food Products, S.A."

"Except it's not flour." Fredo scraped his finger against Coop's shirt and held it up to Kyle's lips.

"That shit would ruin pancakes," he said. "How many more like these?"

"We counted ten."

"How many rooms did you get to?" Fredo asked.

"About thirty."

"Jeez, that's not fast enough. We'll be here for hours, and we don't have that much time, Kyle," said Coop.

"We could pull the fire alarm or the smoke alarm on the incinerator," offered T.J.

"I had Tucker see if he could manually open the hatch, but that will set off an alarm, I fear."

"No problem," Fredo and Coop said in unison.

Kyle called him. "You have any luck?"

The reception was scratchy, but Tucker barked back, "You bet. Ready when you are."

"Okay, count to ten and then let 'er rip." He addressed the crew. "T.J., you and I will watch who comes out, and Fredo, engage the alarms, both of them."

"I'm on it."

Within thirty seconds, a yellow flashing light and ringing alarm blared loudly, followed by the *swoop swoop* of the fire alarm. On the other side of the bank of rooms came the loud buzzer of the cargo bay door as it opened.

Several men started piling out of the rooms, most of them in pajamas and flipflops. Kyle and T.J. hid in a storage closet and watched the shouts and orders begin as men began to clean up the mess and disable the alarms. A huge gust of wind from the open hatch blew napkins all over the area.

Fredo and Coop piled their arms with sheets and hid themselves as they walked past Kyle and T.J. Nearby, Tucker helped to gather some of the errant potato salad bins. Discretely, Kyle checked all the rooms he could, while the other three listened through doors for any sounds of the girls.

They couldn't find anything.

Kyle's phone rang. Antonini's voice sounded angry. "What's going on?"

"Just a little distraction. You better send someone down to help organize the cleanup. Sorry." He hung up and motioned for them to begin checking another bank of crew cabins that had not opened.

One by one, they found the cabins empty.

He dialed Trace.

"We got nothing. But we can't get into the Guest Services area, and they have a casino manager who looks like he played pro football, and he's watching us like a hawk. It's going to take more than a KA-BAR or a passkey to open those areas. Probably where all the money is stored."

"Yeah. Ask him if he's seen a couple of minor girls. That would be his job to notice that."

Trace reported back no.

"We're going to go to the auditorium and check that out. There are catwalks all over the place there and some rooms backstage."

"Good idea. Okay, I'll call you back soon."

"Damn," whispered Fredo. "Now what?"

Kyle had an idea. He called the captain again.

"Your engineer. Did he have a room down with the crew or elsewhere?"

"Eighth floor. Just a minute." Kyle could hear rustling of paperwork. "He was in 807, right next to Dr. Bonelli at 809."

"Thanks." He turned to his other men. "T.J. and Coop, come with me. We're going to pay a little visit to the doctor's quarters on Deck 8. Fredo, you and Tucker keep checking doors and start asking the men if they've seen any girls about. And take more pictures of the pallets in the back. Ask someone when they came on board, if they'll tell you."

"Sure thing."

Kyle and the two medics didn't wait for the elevator, instead racing up the six floors, checked which side the odd numbers were, and approached cabin 807. He leaned next to the door and heard the sounds of sniffling. He smiled and nodded.

"Wish Trace was here," whispered Coop.

"T.J., bust open 809 when I get inside this one." Kyle touched the plastic card to the sensor on the door, heard the click, and turned the handle.

Both Clover and Rebecca looked up in horror and then melted when they saw Kyle's face. When they heard the sounds of the door next to them being demolished, they panicked again.

Coop fell to his knees, removing the ropes that held their hands and feet together, while Kyle removed the dirty rags in their mouths. Clover was crying compulsively, but Rebecca looked nearly comatose.

"They drugged her because she wouldn't stop thrashing," said Clover.

"Are you hurt?" asked Coop.

"N-No, but they said they were going to cut us up and feed us to the sharks!" Clover shouted.

"Shhh," Kyle said, placing his hand on her head.

"You guys are safe. So no one hurt you, either of you?" Kyle's gaze moved back and forth between the two girl's faces. He could see that, out of the two of them, Rebecca was far more traumatized. Her eyes were rolling back in her head, and she began to pass out.

Cooper lifted her up. "We gotta get out of here. I want to check her out. I think she might be having a reaction to the sedative they gave her."

T.J. entered the room, his hands bloody. "The doc's been dead a couple of days, Kyle. They slit his throat."

"Can you walk, honey?" Kyle asked Clover.

She rubbed the redness on her wrists and leaned against him. "We're fine. I want to see my mom."

"No problem."

"I'm going to call Trace," said T.J.

Kyle put the phone to his ear as he guided Clover through the crowd of pajama-clad passengers who had congregated in the hallway. "Fredo, we got them. Come home."

He'd almost forgotten to call Captain Antonini.

"Sir, mission accomplished, but whomever looked for your doctor didn't look very hard. Someone slit his throat and left him in his room. Been dead a couple of days, sorry to say."

He texted Christy, 'Got them. Miss you. Can I sign up for the quiet room?'

CHAPTER 21

T HE *ROMANCIA ITALIANA* was forced to stop in Cabo San Lucas so the Federal Ministerial Police could evaluate the crime scene, remove the body of Dr. Bonelli, and interview the captain, crew, Kyle, and his men. It left Kyle a little nervous to hang around longer than necessary, since he had no desire to encounter General Cortez, who had a running tab with Kyle.

The two governments would be working jointly on the contraband cargo. Several other crew members were also arrested. The cruise line would be fined and their license suspended for a period of months, or perhaps a year. The ongoing investigation against the cartel who arranged the shipment would take just as long, or perhaps longer.

The passengers were given three days at a resort in Cabo and a plane ticket back to San Diego. While some of the passengers took the apology gift, all of the SEALs elected to go home and took just the plane tickets. It was impossible to get everyone on one flight, so they were split up, which was a major disappointment. They all laughed at that. The adventure had been just that, an adventure, but not being able to come home together, well, that was a sacrilege.

Kyle arranged for a get-together on the beach at Coronado the weekend after they got back.

He'd checked in with Captain Antonini after he got home and got the address of the clinic he would be staying at in Sonoma County. He mentioned he had friends who lived up there and perhaps would visit, if the captain allowed it.

He reluctantly did.

"So where did your engineer go?"

"I believe he didn't want to be arrested, so he arranged for someone else to transport the girls to the buyer they had procured online. Turns out, they had been doing this on my ship for many months. They would take pictures of young girls in their bathing suits, find a buyer, and then kidnap them after they got home. Since it wasn't very frequent, it slipped under everyone's radar. The fellow who replaced my chief engineer was a new hire we picked up in Cabo, and of course, he was arrested at the stop."

"Well, I have it on good authority, Uncle Sam thanks you for helping to keep the waterways safe and keeping drugs out of the hands of our citizens. I was told to personally thank you."

"I appreciate that. No medals, of course."

"Of course."

"And the girls are fine? No lasting effects?"

"Someone administered a drug from Dr. Bonelli's office and apparently didn't have the proper experience. He overdosed the younger one, but our medics were able to get her stable to fly her home. And no, they were not touched. The paying customer, you see, was paying for two virgins."

"Despicable. My apologies to the mother and father. I wish I had known."

"I will tell them." He paused, uncomfortable about saying the "G" word, so he signed off with, "Until we meet again, Captain. You focus on your health and I'll try to get up there soon."

"Please do it before I begin to look like Frankenstein."

"It's a promise."

THE BONFIRE WAS soothing and just what they needed. Kyle was happy to see Armando and Gina attend. They were trying again for another baby and seemed to be focusing on their future, not what hadn't happened in their past. He wished them well.

They gathered around the stones when the embers began to fade. Someone had the bright idea about going on another vacation together, which was met with a resounding no by the women, but the men of SEAL Team 3 were game for it.

"It kind of was the perfect vacation, in a way," said Danny. "We got some sun and did some shopping. The kids had a great time, especially that last night with the slumber party. My kids can't wait. We got to have a little action, and we got to save the day. What could be better?"

"No ships, please," said Christy. She got a toast.

"But we did do Gunny proud. And we did it before all the other crap started," said T.J.

"Did everyone come home with all their luggage?" Kyle asked, and the crowd laughed.

"How about we go glamping? We rent those cute fifties-style trailers, all tricked out in period stuff. We go somewhere up to the Redwoods or somewhere on the Oregon coast. Yosemite maybe. It would be cool," said Coop.

"We could go to a dude ranch. The kids would love that too," said Libby.

"I'd rather do that with y'all and leave the men behind," said Shannon, which drew laughter.

"Seriously, guys, the odds of doing another cruise and having something happen again are pretty danged small," said Jameson. "I kinda liked it. I think we'll try one again. What do you say, Lizzie?"

"After the baby, sweetheart. About five years after," Lizzie answered.

"Well, I just remember one of the first things Kyle told me when we started dating. He said we party with the good times, because we never know how long or short that good time will be. We just enjoy it."

"Hear! Hear!" the group said in return.

"I can't imagine what others would think if they knew what we did," said Jake.

"It makes me happy just to see people able to live in a country, even when they do dumb stuff. We're the guys who get 'er done. I wouldn't have it any other way," Kyle said and kissed his bride.

"Hear! Hear!" came the resounding agreement. Some said, "That's a big A-men!"

Did you enjoy your adventure with Kyle and Christy and the other members of SEAL Team 3? Stay tuned for the other three books planned in this new SEAL Brotherhood: Legacy series, all releasing this year— Coop and Libby's story in *Honor The Fallen*, followed by *Grave Injustice* with Gina and Armando, and then *Deal with the Devil*, the story of Nick and Devon, who now own a lavender farm in Sonoma County.

You can find out about these stories here:
SEAL Brotherhood: Legacy
authorsharonhamilton.com/seal-brotherhood-legacy

And read the latest Bone Frog Bachelor book: Unleashed, which releases 2/23/21. Or the prequel, Bone Frog Bachelor, already out, which will give you a great background for this couple.

ABOUT THE AUTHOR

 NYT and USA Today best-selling author Sharon Hamilton's award-winning Navy SEAL Brotherhood series have been a fan favorite from the day the first one was released. They've earned her the coveted Amazon author ranking of #1 in Romantic Suspense, Military Romance and Contemporary Romance categories, as well as in Gothic Romance for her Vampires of Tuscany and Guardian Angels. Her characters follow a sometimes rocky road to redemption through passion and true love.

Now that he's out of the Navy, Sharon can share with her readers that her son spent a decade as a Navy SEAL, and he's the inspiration for her books.

Her Golden Vampires of Tuscany are not like any vamps you've read about before, since they don't go to ground and can walk around in the full light of the sun.

Her Guardian Angels struggle with the human charges they are sent to save, often escaping their vanilla world of Heaven for the brief human one. You won't find any of these beings in any Sunday school class.

She lives in Sonoma County, California with her husband and her Doberman, Tucker. A lifelong organic gardener, when she's not writing, she's getting *verra verra* dirty in the mud, or wandering Farmers Markets looking for new Heirloom varieties of vegetables and flowers. She and her husband plan to cure their wanderlust (or make it worse) by traveling in their Diesel Class A Pusher, Romance Rider. Starting with this book, all her writing will be done on the road.

She loves hearing from her fans:
Sharonhamilton2001@gmail.com

Her website is:
sharonhamiltonauthor.com

Find out more about Sharon, her upcoming releases, appearances and news when you sign up for Sharon's newsletter.

Facebook:
facebook.com/SharonHamiltonAuthor

Twitter:
twitter.com/sharonlhamilton

Pinterest:
pinterest.com/AuthorSharonH

Amazon:
amazon.com/Sharon-Hamilton/e/B004FQQMAC

BookBub:
bookbub.com/authors/sharon-hamilton

Youtube:
youtube.com/channel/UCDInkxXFpXp_4Vnq08ZxMBQ

Soundcloud:
soundcloud.com/sharon-hamilton-1

Sharon Hamilton's Rockin' Romance Readers:
facebook.com/groups/sealteamromance

Sharon Hamilton's Goodreads Group:
goodreads.com/group/show/199125-sharon-hamilton-readers-group

Visit Sharon's Online Store:
sharon-hamilton-author.myshopify.com

Join Sharon's Review Teams:

eBook Reviews:
sharonhamiltonassistant@gmail.com

Audio Reviews:
sharonhamiltonassistant@gmail.com

Life *is one fool thing after another.*
Love *is two fool things after each other.*

REVIEWS

"Well to say the least I was thoroughly surprise. I have read many Vampire books, from Ann Rice to Kym Grosso and few other Authors, so yes I do like Vampires, not the super scary ones from the old days, but the new ones are far more interesting far more human than one can remember. I found Honeymoon Bite a totally engrossing book, I was not able to put it down, page after page I found delight, love, understanding, well that is until the bad bad Vamp started being really bad. But seeing someone love another person so much that they would do anything to protect them, well that had me going, then well there was more and for a while I thought it was the end of a beautiful love story that spanned not only time but, spanned Italy and California. Won't divulge how it ended, but I did shed a few tears after screaming but Sharon Hamilton did not let me down, she took me on amazing trip that I loved, look forward to reading another Vampire book of hers."

"An excellent paranormal romance that was exciting, romantic, entertaining and very satisfying to read. It had me anticipating what would happen next many times over, so much so I could not put it down and even finished it up in a day. The vampires in this book were different from your average vampire, but I enjoy different variations and changes to the same old stuff. It made for a more unpredictable read and more adventurous to explore! Vampire lovers, any paranormal readers and even those who love the romance genre will enjoy Honeymoon Bite."

"This is the first non-Seal book of this author's I have read and I loved it. There is a cast-like hierarchy in this vampire community with humans at the very bottom and Golden vampires at the top. Lionel is a dark vampire who are servants of the Goldens. Phoebe is a Golden who has not decided if she will remain human or accept the turning to become a vampire. Either way she and Lionel can never be together since it is forbidden.

I enjoyed this story and I am looking forward to the next installment."

"A hauntingly romantic read. Old love lost and new love found. Family, heart, intrigue and vampires. Grabbed my attention and couldn't put down. Would definitely recommend."

PRAISE FOR THE
SEAL BROTHERHOOD SERIES

"Fans of Navy SEAL romance, I found a new author to feed your addiction. Finely written and loaded delicious with moments, Sharon Hamilton's storytelling satisfies like a thick bar of chocolate." —Marliss Melton, bestselling author of the *Team Twelve* Navy SEALs series

"Sharon Hamilton does an EXCELLENT job of fitting all the characters into a brotherhood of SEALS that may not be real but sure makes you feel that you have entered the circle and security of their world. The stories intertwine with each book before...and each book after and THAT is what makes Sharon Hamilton's SEAL Brotherhood Series so very interesting. You won't want to put down ANY of her books and they will keep you reading into the night when you should be sleeping. Start with this book...and you will not want to stop until you've read the whole series and then...you will be waiting for Sharon to write the next one." (5 Star Review)

"Kyle and Christy explode all over the pages in this first book, *[Accidental SEAL]*, in a whole new series of SEALs. If the twist and turns don't get your heart jumping, then maybe the suspense will. This is a must read for those that are looking for love and adventure with a little sloppy love thrown in for good measure." (5 Star Review)

PRAISE FOR THE
BAD BOYS OF SEAL TEAM 3 SERIES

"I love reading this series! Once you start these books, you can hardly put them down. The mix of romance and suspense keeps you turning the pages one right after another! Can't wait until the next book!" (5 Star Review)

"I love all of Sharon's Seal books, but *[SEAL's Code]* may just be her best to date. Danny and Luci's journey is filled with a wonderful insight into the Native American life. It is a love story that will fill you with warmth and contentment. You will enjoy Danny's journey to become a SEAL and his reasons for it. Good job Sharon!" (5 Star Review)

PRAISE FOR THE
BAND OF BACHELORS SERIES

"*[Lucas]* was the first book in the Band of Bachelors series and it was a phenomenal start. I loved how we got to see the other SEALs we all love and we got a look at Lucas and Marcy. They had an instant attraction, and their love was very intense. This book had it all, suspense, steamy romance, humor, everything you want in a riveting, outstanding read. I can't wait to read the next book in this series." (5 Star Review)

PRAISE FOR THE
TRUE BLUE SEALS SERIES

"Keep the tissues box nearby as you read *True Blue SEALs: Zak* by Sharon Hamilton. I imagine more than I wish to that the circumstances surrounding Zak and Amy are all too real for returning military personnel and their families. Ms. Hamilton has put us right in the middle of struggles and successes that these two high school sweethearts endure. I have read several of Sharon Hamilton's military romances but will say this is the most emotionally intense of the ones that I have read. This is a well-written, realistic story with authentic characters that will have you rooting for them and proud of those who serve to keep us safe. This is an author who writes amazing stories that you love and cry with the characters. Fans of Jessica Scott and Marliss Melton will want to add Sharon Hamilton to their list of realistic military romance writers." (5 Star Review)

"Dear FATHER IN HEAVEN,

If I may respectfully say so sometimes you are a strange God. Though you love all mankind,

It seems you have special predilections too.

You seem to love those men who can stand up alone who face impossible odds, Who challenge every bully and every tyrant ~

Those men who know the heat and loneliness of Calvary. Possibly you cherish men of this stamp because you recognize the mark of your only son in them.

Since this unique group of men known as the SEALs know Calvary and suffering, teach them now the mystery of the resurrection ~ that they are indestructible, that they will live forever because of their deep faith in you.

And when they do come to heaven, may I respectfully warn you, Dear Father, they also know how to celebrate. So please be ready for them when they insert under your pearly gates.

Bless them, their devoted Families and their Country on this glorious occasion.

We ask this through the merits of your Son, Christ Jesus the Lord, Amen."

By Reverend E.J. McMalhon S.J. LCDR, CHC, USN
Awards Ceremony SEAL Team One
1975 At NAB, Coronado

Made in the USA
Coppell, TX
17 August 2022